The death machines are capable of any treachery, able to assume any disguise, motivated only by their prime directive: to seek out and destroy life wherever it may hide.

MAN

The fragile life-form that hides within its puny frame a curiously unquenchable something . . . call it 'spirit'. This odd facet of an otherwise undistinguished example of the disease of life has been a source of deep annoyance to the berserkers since first the two forms met: no wonder then that for each the other is

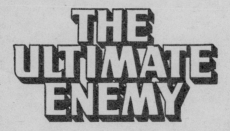

BERSERKERS

FRED SABERHAGEN

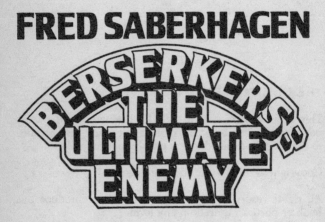

BERSERKERS: THE ULTIMATE ENEMY

BAEN BOOKS

THE ULTIMATE ENEMY

This is a work of fiction. All the characters and events portrayed in this book are fictional, and any resemblance to real people or incidents is purely coincidental.

A Baen Book

Baen Publishing Enterprises
260 Fifth Avenue
New York, N.Y. 10001

First Baen printing, June 1988

ISBN: 0-671-65414-4

Cover art by David Martin

Printed in the United States of America

Distributed by
SIMON & SCHUSTER
1230 Avenue of the Americas
New York, N.Y. 10020

CONTENTS

Acknowledgments

THE SMILE: Copyright © 1977, Algol Magazine. First appeared in Algol, Summer/Fall 1977.

PRESSURE: Copyright © 1967, Galaxy Publishing Corp. First appeared (as "Berserker's Prey") in Worlds of If, June 1977.

THE ANNIHILATION OF ANGKOR APEIRON: Copyright © 1974, UPD Publishing Corp. First appeared in Galaxy, Feb. 1975.

INHUMAN ERROR: Copyright © 1974, Conde Nast Publications, Inc. First appeared in Analog, Oct. 1974.

SOME EVENTS AT THE TEMPLAR RADIANT: Copyright © 1979, Fred Saberhagen. First appeared in Destinies, May-Aug. 1979.

STARSONG: Copyright © 1967, Galaxy Publishing Corp. First appeared in Worlds of If, Jan. 1968.

SMASHER: Copyright © 1978, Mercury Press Inc. First appeared in The Magazine of Fantasy and Science Fiction. Aug. 1978.

THE GAME: Copyright © 1977, Fred Saberhagen. First appeared in The Flying Buffalo's Favorite Magazine, May-June 1977.

WINGS OUT OF SHADOW: Copyright © 1974, UPD Publishing Corp. First appeared in Worlds of If, March-April 1974.

Once more I, Third historian of the Carmpan race, thankful to Earth-descended humans for their defense of my world and of many worlds, have recorded for them a series of my visions. Relatively unfettered by time or space, my mind has roamed the Galaxy in past and future to gather pieces of the truth of the great war of life against unliving death. What I have set down is far from the whole truth of that war, yet it is true.

Most of the higher intellects of the galaxy will shrink from war, even when survival depends upon it absolutely. Yet from the same matter that supports their lives, came the berserkers. Were their Builders uniquely evil? Would that it were so . . .

THE SMILE

The berserker attack upon the world called St. Gervase had ended some four standard months before the large and luxurious private yacht of the Tyrant Yoritomo appeared amid the ashclouds and rainclouds that still monotonized the planet's newly lifeless sky. From the yacht a silent pair of waspish-looking launches soon began a swift descent, to land on the denuded surface where the planet's capital city had once stood.

The crews disembarking from the launches were armored against hot ash and hot mud and residual radiation. They knew what they were looking for, and in less than a standard hour they had located the vaulted tunnel leading down, from what had been a sub-basement of the famed St. Gervase Museum.

1

The tunnel was partially collapsed in places, but still passable, and they followed its steps downward, stumbling here and there on debris fallen from the surface. The battle had not been completely one-sided in its early stages, and scattered amid the wreckage of the once-great city were fragments of berserker troop-landers and of their robotic shock-troops. The unliving metal killers had had to force a landing, to neutralize the defensive field generators, before the bombardment could begin in earnest.

The tunnel terminated in a large vault a hundred meters down. The lights, on an independent power supply, were still working, and the air conditioning was still trying to keep out dust. There were five great statues in the vault, including one in the attached workshop where some conservator or restorer had evidently been treating it. Each one was a priceless masterwork. And scattered in an almost casual litter throughout the shelter were paintings, pottery, small works in bronze and gold and silver, the least a treasure to be envied.

At once the visitors radioed news of their discovery to one who waited eagerly in the yacht hovering above. Their report concluded with the observation that someone had evidently been living down here since the attack. Beside the workshop, with its power lamp to keep things going, there was a small room that had served as a repository of the Museum's records. A cot stood in it now, there had been food supplies laid in, and there were other signs of human habitation. Well, it was not too strange that there should have been a few survivors, out of a population of many millions.

The man who had been living alone in the shelter

for four months came back to find the landing party going busily about their work.

"Looters," he remarked, in a voice that seemed to have lost the strength for rage, or even fear. Not armored against radiation or anything else, he leaned against the terminal doorway of the battered tunnel, a long-haired, unshaven, once-fat man whose frame was now swallowed up in clothes that looked as if they might not have been changed since the attack.

The member of the landing party standing nearest looked back at him silently, and drummed fingers on the butt of a holstered handgun, considering. The man who had just arrived threw down the pieces of metallic junk he had brought with him, conveying in the gesture his contempt.

The handgun was out of its holster, but before it was leveled, an intervention from the leader of the landing party came in the form of a sharp gesture. Without taking his eyes off the man in the doorway, the leader at once reopened communication with the large ship waiting above.

"Your Mightiness, we have a survivor here," he informed the round face that soon appeared upon the small portable wallscreen. "I believe it is the sculptor Antonio Nobrega."

"Let me see him at once. Bring him before the screen." The voice of His Mightiness was inimitable and terrible, and no less terrible, somehow, because he always sounded short of breath. "Yes, you are right, although he is much changed. Nobrega, how fortunate for us both! This is indeed another important find."

"I knew you would be coming to St. Gervase now," Nobrega told the screen, in his empty voice. "Like a disease germ settling in a mangled body.

Like some great fat cancer virus. Did you bring along your woman, to take charge of our Culture?"

One of the men beside the sculptor knocked him down. A breathless little snarl came from the screen at this, and Nobrega was quickly helped back to his feet, then put into a chair.

"He is an artist, my faithful ones," the screen-voice chided. "We must not expect him to have any sense of the fitness of things outside his art. No. We must get the maestro here some radiation treatment, and then bring him along with us to the Palace, and he will live and work there as happily, or unhappily, as elsewhere."

"Oh no," said the artist from his chair, more faintly than before. "My work is done."

"Pish-posh. You'll see."

"I knew you were coming . . ."

"Oh?" The small voice from the screen was humoring him. "And how did you know that?"

"I heard . . . when our fleet was still defending the approaches to the system, my daughter was out there with it. Through her, before she died, I heard how you brought your own fleet in-system, to watch what was going to happen, to judge our strength, our chance of resisting the berserkers. I heard how your force vanished when they came. I said then that you'd be back, to loot the things you could never get at in any other way."

Nobrega was quiet for a moment, then lunged from his chair—or made the best attempt at lunging that he could. He grabbed up a long metal sculptor's tool and drew it back to swing at *Winged Truth Rising*, a marble Poniatowski eleven centuries old. "Before I'll see you take this—"

Before he could knock a chip of marble loose, he was overpowered, and put into restraint.

When they approached him again an hour later, to take him up to the yacht for medical examination and treatment, they found him already dead. Autopsy on the spot discovered several kinds of slow and gentle poison. Nobrega might have taken some deliberately. Or he might have been finished by something the berserkers had left behind, to ensure that there would be no survivors, as they moved on to carry out their programmed task of eradicating all life from the Galaxy.

On his voyage home from St. Gervase, and for several months thereafter, Yoritomo was prevented by pressing business from really inspecting his new treasures. By then the five great statues had been installed, to good esthetic advantage, in the deepest, largest, and best-protected gallery of the Palace. Lesser collections had been evicted to make room and visual space for *Winged Truth Rising*; Lazamon's *Laughing* (or *Raging*) *Bacchus*; *The Last Provocation*, by Sarapion; Lazienki's *Twisting Room*; and *Remembrance of Past Wrongs*, by Prajapati.

It chanced that at this time the Lady Yoritomo was at the Palace too. Her duties, as Cultural Leader of the People, and High Overseer of Education for the four tributary planets, kept her on the move, and it often happened that she and her Lord did not see each other for a month or longer at a time.

The two of them trusted each other more than they trusted anyone else. Today they sat alone in the great gallery and sipped tea, and spoke of business.

The Lady was trying to promote her latest theory, which was that love for the ruling pair might be implanted genetically in the next generation of people on the tributary worlds. Several experimental projects had already begun. So far these had achieved little but severe mental retardation in the subjects, but there were plenty of new subjects and she was not discouraged.

The Lord spoke mainly of his own plan, which was to form a more explicit working arrangement with the berserkers. In this scheme the Yoritomos would furnish the killer machines with human lives they did not need, and planets hard to defend, in exchange for choice works of art and, of course, immunity from personal attack. The plan had many attractive features, but the Lord had to admit that the difficulty of opening negotiations with berserkers, let alone establishing any degree of mutual trust, made it somewhat impractical.

When a pause came in the conversation, Yoritomo had the banal thought that he and his wife had little to talk about anymore, outside of business. With a word to her, he rose from the alcove where they had been sitting, and walked to the far end of the gallery of statues to replenish the tea pot. For esthetic reasons he refused to allow robots in here; nor did he want human servitors around while this private discussion was in progress. Also, he thought, as he retraced his steps, the Lady could not help but be flattered, and won toward his own position in a certain matter where they disagreed, when she was served personally by the hands of one so mighty . . .

He rounded the great metal flank of *The Last Provocation* and came to a dumb halt, in shocked surprise so great that for a moment his facial expression did not even alter. Half a minute ago he had left her vivacious and thoughtful and full of graceful energy. She was still in the same place, on the settee, but slumped over sideways now, one arm extended with its slender, jeweled finger twitching upon the rich brown carpet. The Lady's hair was wildly disarranged; and small wonder, he thought madly, for her *head* had been twisted almost completely around, so her dead eyes now looked over one bare shoulder almost straight at Yoritomo. Upon her shoulder and her cheek were bruised discolorations . . .

He spun around at last, dropping the fragile masterpiece that held his tea. His concealed weapon was half-drawn before it was smashed out of his grip. He had one look at death, serenely towering above him. He had not quite time enough to shriek, before the next blow fell.

The wind had not rested in the hours since Ritwan's arrival, and with an endless howl it drove the restless land before it. He could quite easily believe that in a few years the great pit left by the destruction of the old Yoritomo Palace had been completely filled. The latest dig had ended only yesterday, and already the archaeologists' fresh pits were beginning to be reoccupied by sand.

"They were actually more pirates than anything else," Iselin, the chief archaeologist, was saying. "At the peak of their power two hundred years ago they ruled four systems. Ruled them from here, though there's not much showing on the surface now but this old sandpile."

"Ozymandias," Ritwan murmured.

"What?"

"An ancient poem." He pushed back sandy hair from his forehead with a thin, nervous hand. "I wish

I'd got here in time to see the statues before you crated them and stowed them on your ship. You can imagine I came as fast as I could from Sirgol, when I heard there was a dig in progress here."

"Well." Iselin folded her plump arms and frowned, then smiled, a white flash in a dark Indian face. "Why don't you ride with us back to Esteel system? I really can't open the crates for anything until we get there. Not under the complicated rules of procedure we're stuck with on these jointly sponsored digs."

"My ship does have a good autopilot."

"Then set it to follow ours, and hop aboard. When we unpack on Esteel you can be among the first to look your fill. Meanwhile we can talk. I wish you'd been with us all along, we've missed having a really first-rate art historian."

"All right, I'll come." They offered each other enthusiastic smiles. "It's true, then, you really found most of the old St. Gervase collection intact?"

"I don't know that we can claim that. But there's certainly a lot."

"Just lying undisturbed here, for about two centuries."

"Well, as I say, this was the Yoritomos' safe port. But it looks like no more than a few thousand people ever lived on this world at any one time, and no one at all has lived here for a considerable period. Some intrigue or other evidently started among the Tyrant's lieutenants—no one's ever learned exactly how or why it started, but the thieves fell out. There was fighting, the Palace destroyed, the rulers themselves killed, and the whole thing collapsed. None of the intriguers had the ability to keep it going, I suppose, with the so-called Lord and Lady gone."

"Just when was that?"

Iselin named a date.

"The same year St. Gervase fell. That fits. The Yoritomos could have gone there after the berserkers left, and looted at their leisure. That would fit with their character, wouldn't it?"

"I'm afraid so . . . you see, the more I learned of them, the more I felt sure that they must have had a deeper, more secret shelter than any that was turned up in the early digs a century ago. The thing is, the people who dug here then found so much loot they were convinced they'd found it all."

Ritwan was watching the pits fill slowly in.

Iselin gave his arm a friendly shake. "And—did I tell you? We found two skeletons, I think of the Yoritomos themselves. Lavishly dressed in the midst of their greatest treasures. Lady died of a broken neck, and the man of multiple . . ."

The wind was howling still, when the two ships lifted off.

Aboard ship on the way to Esteel, things were relaxed and pleasant, if just a trifle cramped. With Ritwan along, they were six on board, and had to fit three to a cabin in narrow bunks. It was partially the wealth of the find that crowded them, of course. There were treasures almost beyond imagining stowed in plastic cratings almost everywhere one looked. The voyagers could expect a good deal of leisure time en route to marvel at it all. Propulsion and guidance and life-support were taken care of by machinery, with just an occasional careful human glance by way of circumspection. People in this particular portion of the inhabited Galaxy traveled now, as they had two hundred years before, in relative security from berserker attack. And now there were no human pirates.

Lashed in place in the central cargo bay stood the five great, muffled forms from which Ritwan particularly yearned to tear the pads and sheeting. But he made himself be patient. On the first day out he joined the others in the cargo bay, where they watched and listened to some of the old recordings found in the lower ruins of the Yoritomo Palace. There were data stored on tapes, in crystal cubes, around old permafrozen circuit rings. And much of the information was in the form of messages recorded by the Tyrant himself.

"The Gods alone know why he recorded this one," sighed Oshogbo. She was chief archivist of a large Esteel museum, one of the expedition's sponsoring institutions. "Listen to this. Look at him. He's ordering a ship to stand by and be boarded, or face destruction."

"The ham actor in him, maybe," offered Chinan, who on planet had been an assistant digger for the expedition, but in space became its captain. "He needed to study his delivery."

"Every one of his ships could carry the recording," suggested Klyuchevski, expert excavator. "So their victims wouldn't know if the Tyrant himself were present or not—I'm not sure how much difference it would make."

"Let's try another," said Granton, chief record-keeper and general assistant.

Within the next hour they sampled recordings in which Yoritomo: (1) ordered his subordinates to stop squabbling over slaves and concubines; (2) pleaded his case, to the Interworlds Government, as that of a man unjustly maligned, the representative of a persecuted people; (3) conducted a video tour, for some supposed audience whose identity was never made clear, of the most breathtaking parts of his vast collection of art . . .

"Wait!" Ritwan broke in. "What was that bit? Would you run that last part once more?"

The Tyrant's asthmatic voice repeated: "The grim story of how these magnificent statues happened to be saved. Our fleet had made every effort but still arrived *too* late to be of any help to the heroic defenders of St. Gervase. For many days we searched in vain for survivors; we found just one. And this man's identity made the whole situation especially poignant to me, for it was the sculptor Antonio Nobrega. Sadly, our help had come too late, and he shortly succumbed to the berserker poisons. I hope that the day will come soon, when all governments will heed my repeated urgings, to prosecute a war to the finish against these scourges of . . ."

"So!" Ritwan looked pleased, a man who has just had an old puzzle solved for him. "That's where Nobrega died, then. We've thought for some time it was likely—most of his family was there—but we had no hard evidence before."

"He was the famous forger, wasn't he?" asked Granton.

"Yes. A really good artist in his own right, though the shady side of his work has somewhat overshadowed the rest." Ritwan allowed time for the few small groans earned by the pun, and went on: "I'd hate to accept the old Tyrant's word on anything. But I suppose he'd have no reason to lie about Nobrega."

Iselin was looking at her wrist. "Lunch time for

me. Maybe the rest of you want to spend all day in here."

"I can resist recordings." Ritwan got up to accompany her. "Now, if you were opening up the crates—"

"No chance, friend. But I can show you holograms—didn't I mention that?"

"You didn't!"

Oshogbo called after them: "Here's the Lord and Lady both, on this one—"

They did not stop. Chi-nan came out with them, leaving three people still in the cargo bay.

In the small ship's lounge, the three who had left set up lunch with a floor show.

"This is really decadence. Pea soup with ham, and—what have we here? Lazienki. Marvelous!"

The subtle grays and reds of *Twisting Room* (was it the human heart?) came into existence, projected by hidden devices in the corners of the lounge, and filling up the center. Iselin with a gesture made the full-size image rotate slowly.

"Captain?" the intercom asked hoarsely, breaking in.

"I knew it—just sit down, and—"

"I think we have some kind of cargo problem here." It sounded like Granton's voice, perturbed. "Something seems to be breaking up, or . . . Iselin, you'd better come too, and take a look at your . . ."

A pause, with background smashing noises. Then incoherent speech, in mixed voices, ending in a hoarse cry.

Chi-nan was already gone. Ritwan, sprinting, just kept in sight of Iselin's back going around corners. Then she stopped so suddenly that he almost ran into her.

The doorway to the cargo hold, left wide open when they came out of it a few minutes before, was now sealed tightly by a massive sliding door, a safety door designed to isolate compartments in case of emergencies like fire or rupture of the hull.

On the deck just outside the door, a human figure sprawled. Iselin and Chi-nan were already crouched over it; as Ritwan bent over them, a not-intrinsically-unpleasant smell of scorched meat reached his nostrils.

"Help me lift her . . . careful . . . sick bay's that way."

Ritwan helped Iselin. Chi-nan sprang to his feet, looked at an indicator beside the heavy door, and momentarily rested a hand on its flat surface.

"Something burning in there," he commented tersely, and then came along with the others on the quick hustle to sickbay. At his touch the small door opened for them, lights springing on inside.

"What's in our cargo that's not fireproofed?" Iselin demanded, as if all this were some personal insult hurled her way by Fate.

Dialogue broke off for a while. The burn-tank, hissing brim-full twenty seconds after the proper studs were punched, received Oshogbo's scorched dead weight, clothes and all, and went to work upon her with a steady sloshing. Then, while Iselin stayed in sick bay, Ritwan followed Chi-nan on another scrambling run, back to the small bridge. There the captain threw himself into an acceleration chair and laid swift hands on his controls, demanding an accounting from his ship.

In a moment he had switched his master intercom to show conditions inside the cargo bay, where two people were still unaccounted for. On the deck in there lay something clothed, a bundle-of-old-rags sort of something. In the remaining moment of clear vision before the cargo bay pickup went dead, Ritwan and Chi-nan both glimpsed a towering, moving shape.

The captain stared for a moment at the gray noise which came next, then switched to sick bay. Iselin appeared at once.

"How's she doing?" Chi-nan demanded.

"Signs are stabilizing. She's got a crack in the back of her skull as well as the burns on her torso, the printout says. As if something heavy had hit her in the head."

"Maybe the door clipped her, sliding closed, just as she got out." The men in the control room could see into the tank, and the captain raised his voice. "Oshy, can you answer me? What happened to Granton and Klu?"

The back of Oshogbo's neck was cradled on a rest of ivory plastic. Her body shook and shimmied lightly, vibrating with the dark liquid, as if she might be enjoying her swim. Here and there burnt shreds of clothing were now drifting free. She looked around and seemed to be trying to locate Chi-nan's voice. Then she spoke: "It . . . grabbed them. I . . . ran."

"What grabbed them? Are they still alive?"

"Granton's head came . . . it pulled off his head. I got out. Something hit . . ." The young woman's eyes rolled, her voice faded.

Iselin's face came into view again. "She's out of it; I think the medic just put her to sleep. Should I try to get it to wake her again?"

"Not necessary." The captain sounded shaken. "I think we must assume the others are finished. I'm not going to open that door, anyway, until I know more about our problem."

Ritwan asked: "Can we put down on some planet quickly?"

"Not one where we can get help," the captain told him over one shoulder. "There's no help closer than Esteel. Three or four days."

The three of them quickly talked over the problem, agreeing on what they knew. Two people were sure that they had seen, on intercom, something large moving about inside the cargo bay.

"And," Iselin concluded, "our surviving firsthand witness says that 'it' tore off someone's head."

"Sounds like a berserker," Ritwan said impulsively. "Or could it possibly be some animal—? Anyway, how could anything that big have been hiding in there?"

"An animal's impossible," Chi-nan told him flatly. "And you should have seen how we packed that space, how carefully we checked to see if we were wasting any room. The only place anyone or anything *could* have been hidden was inside one of those statuary crates."

Iselin added: "And I certainly checked out every one of them. We formed them to fit closely around the statues, and they couldn't have contained anything else of any size. What's that noise?"

The men in the control room could hear it too, a muffled, rhythmic banging, unnatural for any space ship that Ritwan had ever ridden. He now, for some reason, suddenly thought of what kind of people they had been whose Palace had provided this mysterious cargo; and for the first time since the trouble had started he began to feel real fear.

He put a hand on the other man's shoulder. "Chi-nan—what exactly did we see on the intercom screen?"

The captain thought before answering. "Something

big, taller than a man, anyway. And moving by itself.
Right?"

"Yes, and I'd say it was dark . . . beyond that, I
don't know."

"I would have called it light-colored." The muffled
pounding sounds had grown a little steadier, faster,
louder. "So, do you think one of our statues has
come alive on us?"

Iselin's voice from sick bay offered: "I think 'alive'
is definitely the wrong word."

Ritwan asked: "How many of the statues have
movable joints?" *Twisting Room*, which he had seen
in hologram, did not. But articulated sculpture had
been common enough a few centuries earlier.

"Two did," said Iselin.

"I looked at all the statues closely," Chi-nan pro-
tested. "Iselin, you did too. We all did, naturally.
And they were genuine."

"We never checked inside them, for controls, power
supplies, robotic brains. Did we?"

"Of course not. There was no reason."

Ritwan persisted: "So it is a berserker. It can't be
anything else. And it waited until now to attack,
because it wants to be sure to get the ship."

Chi-nan pounded his chair-arm with a flat hand.
"No! I can't buy that. Do you think that emergency
door would stop a berserker? We'd all be dead now,
and it would have the ship. And you're saying it's a
berserker that looks just like a masterpiece by a great
artist, enough alike to fool experts; and that it stayed
buried there for two hundred years without digging
itself out; and that—"

"Nobrega," Ritwan interrupted suddenly.

"What?"

"Nobrega . . . he died on St. Gervase, we don't

know just how. He had every reason to hate the Yoritomos. Most probably he met one or both of them at the St. Gervase Museum, after the attack, while they were doing what they called their collecting.

"You said Nobrega was a great forger. Correct. A good engineer, too. You also said that no one knows exactly how the Yoritomos came to die, only that their deaths were violent. And occurred among these very statues."

The other two, one on screen and one at hand, were very quiet, watching him.

"Suppose," Ritwan went on, "Nobrega knew somehow that the looters would be coming, and he had the time and the means to concoct something special for them. Take a statue with movable limbs, and build in a power lamp, sensors, controls—a heat-projector, maybe, as a weapon. And then add the electronic brain from some small berserker unit."

Chi-nan audibly sucked in his breath.

"There might easily have been some of those lying around on St. Gervase, after the attack. Everyone agrees it was a fierce defense."

"I'm debating with myself," said Chi-nan, "whether we should all pile into the lifeboat, and head for your ship, Ritwan. It's small, as you say, but I suppose we'd fit, in a pinch."

"There's no real sick bay."

"Oh." They all looked at the face of the young woman in the tank, unconscious now, dark hair dancing round it upon the surface of the healing fluid.

"Anyway," the captain resumed, "I'm not sure it couldn't take over the controls here, catch us, ram us somehow. Maybe, as you think, it's not a real berserker. But it seems to be too close to the real thing to just turn over our ship to it. We're going to have to stay and fight."

"Bravo," said Iselin. "But with what? It seems to me we stowed away our small arms in the cargo bay somewhere."

"We did. Let's hope Nobrega didn't leave it brains enough to look for them, and it just keeps banging on that door. Meanwhile, let's check what digging equipment we can get at."

Iselin decided it was pointless for her to remain in sick bay, and came to help them, leaving the intercom channel open so they could look in on Oshogbo from time to time.

"That door to the cargo bay is denting and bulging, boys," she told them as she ducked into the cramped storage space beneath the lounge where they were rummaging. "Let's get something organized in the way of weapons."

Ritwan grunted, dragging out a long, thick-bodied tool, evidently containing its own power supply. "What's this, an autohammer? Looks like it would do a job."

"Sure," said Chi-nan. "If you get within arm's length. We'll save that for when we're really desperate."

A minute later, digging through boxes of electrical-looking devices strange to Ritwan, the captain murmured: "If he went to all the trouble of forging an old master he must have had good reason. Well, it'd be the one thing the Yoritomos might accept at face value. Take it right onto their ship, into their private rooms. He must have been out to get the Lord and Lady both."

"I guess that was it. I suppose just putting a simple bomb in the statue wouldn't have been sure enough, or selective enough."

"Also it might have had to pass some machines that sniff out explosives, before it got into the inner . . . Ritwan! When that thing attacked, just now, what recording were they listening to in the cargo bay?"

Ritwan stopped in the middle of opening another box. "Oshogbo called it out to us as we were leaving. You're right, one with both the Yoritomos on it. Nobrega must have set his creation to be triggered by their voices, heard together."

"How it's supposed to be turned off, is what I'd like to know."

"It did turn off, for some reason, didn't it? And lay there for two centuries. Probably Nobrega didn't foresee that the statue might survive long enough for the cycle to be able to repeat. Maybe if we can just hold out a little longer, it'll turn itself off again."

Patient and regular as a clock, the muffled battering sounded on.

"Can't depend on that, I'm afraid." Chi-nan kicked away the last crate to be searched. "Well, this seems to be the extent of the hardware we have for putting together weapons. It looks like whatever we use is going to have to be electrical. I think we can rig up something to electrocute—if that's the right word—or fry, or melt, the enemy. We've got to know first, though, just which of those statues is the one we're fighting. There are only two possible mobile ones, which narrows it down. But still."

"*Laughing Bacchus*," Iselin supplied. "And *Remembrance of Past Wrongs*."

"The first is basically steel. We can set up an induction field strong enough to melt it down, I think. A hundred kilos or so of molten iron in the middle of the deck may be hard to deal with, but not as hard as what we've got now. But the other statue, or anyway its outer structure, is some kind of very hard and tough ceramic. That one will need something like a lightning bolt to knock it out." A horrible thought seemed to strike Chi-nan all at once. "You don't suppose there could be *two*—?"

Ritwan gestured reassurance. "I think Nobrega would have put all his time and effort into perfecting one."

"So," said Iselin, "it all comes down to knowing which one he forged, and which is really genuine. The one he worked on must be forged; even if he'd started with a real masterpiece to build his killing device, by the time he got everything implanted the surface would have to be almost totally reconstructed."

"So I'm going up to the lounge," the art historian replied. "And see those holograms. If we're lucky I'll be able to spot it."

Iselin came with him, muttering: "All you have to do, friend, is detect a forgery that got past Yoritomo and *his* experts . . . maybe we'd better think of something else."

In the lounge the holograms of the two statues were soon displayed full size, side by side and slowly rotating. Both were tall, roughly humanoid figures, and both in their own ways were smiling.

A minute and a half had passed when Ritwan said, decisively: "This one's the forgery. Build your lightning device."

Before the emergency door at last gave way under that mindless, punch-press pounding, the electrical equipment had been assembled and moved into place. On either side of the doorway Chi-nan and Iselin crouched, manning their switches. Ritwan (counted the most expendable in combat) stood in plain view opposite the crumpling door, garbed in a heat-insulating spacesuit and clutching the heavy auto-hammer to his chest.

The final failure of the door was sudden. One moment it remained in place, masking what lay beyond; next moment, it had been torn away. For a long second of the new silence, the last work of Antonio Nobrega stood clearly visible, bone-white in the glare of lamps on every side, against the black-ened ruin of what had been the cargo bay.

Ritwan raised the hammer, which suddenly felt no heavier than a microprobe. For a moment he knew what people felt, who face the true berserker foe in combat.

The tall thing took a step toward him, serenely smiling. And the blue-white blast came at it from the side, faster than any mere matter could be made to dodge.

A couple of hours later the most urgent damage-control measures had been taken, two dead bodies had been packed for preservation—with real rever-ence if without gestures—and the pieces of Nobrega's work, torn asunder by the current that the ceramic would not peacefully admit, had cooled enough to handle.

Ritwan had promised to show the others how he had known the forgery; and now he came up with the fragment he was looking for. "This," he said.

"The mouth?"

"The smile. If you've looked at as much Federa-tion era art as I have, the incongruity is obvious. The smile's all wrong for Prajapati's period. It's evil, cunning—when the face was intact you could see it plainly. Gloating. Calm and malevolent at the same time."

Iselin asked: "But Nobrega himself didn't see that? Or Yoritomo?"

"For the period they lived in, the smile's just fine, artistically speaking. They couldn't step forward or backward two hundred years, and get a better perspective. I suppose revenge is normal in any century, but tastes in art are changeable."

Chi-nan said: "I thought perhaps the subject or the title gave you some clue."

"*Remembrance of Past Wrongs*—no, Prajapati did actually do something very similar in subject, as I recall. As I say, I suppose revenge knows no cultural or temporal boundaries."

Normal in any century. Oshogbo, watching via intercom from the numbing hurn-treatment bath, shivered and closed her eyes. *No boundaries.*

The universe has given life its own arsenal of weapons, and I am no longer surprised that even tenderness may sometimes be counted among them. Even the most gentle and humble of living things may demonstrate surprising strength . . .

PRESSURE

The ship had been a human transport once, and it still transported humans, but now they rode like well-cared-for cattle on the road to market. Control of their passage and destiny had been vested in the electronic brain and auxiliary devices built into the *New England* after its capture in space by a berserker machine.

Gilberto Klee, latest captive to be thrust aboard, was more frightened than ever before in his young life, and trying not to show it. Why the berserker had kept him alive at all he did not know, and he was afraid to think about it. Like everyone else he had heard the horror stories—of human brains, still half-alive, built into berserker computers as auxiliary circuits; of human bodies used in the berserkers' experiments intended to produce convincing artificial men; of humans kept as test-targets for new berserker death-rays, toxins, ways to drive men mad.

After the raid Gil and the handful of others who had been taken with him—for all they knew, the only survivors of their planet—had been separated and kept in solitary compartments aboard the great machine in space. And now the same berserker de-vices that had captured him, or others like them, had taken him from his cell and led him to an interior dock aboard the planetoid-sized berserker; and be-fore they put him aboard this ship that had been a human transport once, he had time to see the name *New England* on her hull.

Once aboard, he was put into a chamber about twenty paces wide, perhaps fifty long, twelve or fifteen feet high. Evidently all interior decks and paneling, everything non-essential, had been ripped out. There was left the inner hull, some plumbing, some light, artificial gravity and air at a good level.

There were eight other people in the chamber, standing together and talking among themselves. They fell silent as the machines opened the door and thrust Gil among them.

"How do," said one man to Gil, as the door closed behind the machines again. The speaker was a thin guy who wore some kind of spaceman's uniform that now bagged loosely on his frame. As he spoke he took a cautious step forward and nodded. Everyone was watching Gil alertly—in case he should turn out to be violently crazy, Gil supposed. Well, it wasn't the first time in his life he'd been thrown in with a group of prisoners who looked at him like that.

"My name is Rom," the thin guy was saying. "En-sign Rom, United Planets Space Force."

"Gilberto Klee."

Everyone relaxed just slightly, seeing that he at least sounded normal.

"This is Mr. Hudak," said Ensign Rom, indicating another young, once-authoritative man. Then he went on to name the others, but Gil couldn't remember all their names at once. Three of them were women, one of them young enough to make Gil look at her with some interest. Then he saw how she kept half-crouching behind the other people, staring smiling at nothing, fingers playing unceasingly with her long and unkempt hair.

Mr. Hudak had started to ask Gil questions, his voice gradually taking on the tone used by people-in-charge conducting an examination. In school, Youth Bureau, police station, Resettlement, always there was a certain tone of voice used by the processors when speaking to the processed—though Gil had never put the thought in just those words.

Hudak was asking him: "Were you on another ship, or what?" On a ship. You were not a spaceman, of course, said the tone of authority now. You were just a boy being processed somewhere, we see that by looking at you. Not that the tone of authority was intentionally nasty. It usually wasn't.

"I was on a planet," said Gil. "Bella Coola."

"My God, they hit that too?"

"They sure hit the part where I was, anyway." Gil hadn't seen anything to make him hopeful about the rest of the planet. At the Resettlement Station where he was they had had just a few minutes' warning from the military, and then the radios had gone silent. When the berserker launch came down, Gil had been out in the fields just watching. There wasn't much the people at the Station could do with the little warning they had been given; already they could see the berserker heat-rays and dust-machines playing over the woods, which was the only conceal-ment they might have run to.

Still, some of the kids had been trying to run when the silvery, poisonous-looking dart that was the ber-serker's launch had appeared descending overhead.

The Old Man had come tearing out of the compound into the fields on his scooter—maybe to tell his young people to run, maybe to tell them to stand still. It didn't seem to make much difference. The ones who ran were rayed down by the enemy and the ones who didn't were rounded up. What Gil recalled most clearly about the other kids dying was the look of agony on the Old Man's face—that one face of authority that had never seemed to be looking at Gil from the other side of a glass wall.

When all the survivors of the Station had been herded together, standing in a little crowd under the bright sky in the middle of a vine-grown field, the machines singled out the Old Man.

Some of the machines that had landed were in the shape of metal men, some looked more like giant steel ants. "Thus to all life, save that which serves the cause of Death," said a twanging metal voice. And a steel hand picked a squash from a vine, and held the fruit up and squeezed through it so it fell away in broken pulpy halves. And then the same hand, with squash-pulp still clinging to the bright fingers, reached to take the Old Man by the wrist.

The twanging voice said: "You are in control of these other life-units. You will now order them to cooperate willingly with us."

The Old Man only shook his head, no. Muttered something.

The bright hand squeezed, slowly.

The Old Man screamed, but did not fall. Neither did he give any order for cooperation. Gil was standing rigid, and silent, but screaming in his own mind for the Old Man to give in, to fall down and pass out, anything to make it stop . . .

But the Old Man would not fall, or pass out, or

give the order that was wanted. Not even when the
berserker's big hand came up to clamp around his
skull, and the pressure was once more applied, slowly
as before.

"What was on Bella Coola?" Ensign Rom was asking him "I mean, military—?"

"Not much, I guess," said Gil. "I don't know much
about military stuff. I was just sort of studying to be a
farmer."

"Oh." Rom and Hudak, the two sharp capable-
looking ones among the prisoners, exchanged glances.
Maybe they knew the farms on Bella Coola had been
just a sort of reform-school setup for tough kids from
Earth and other crowded places. Gil told himself he
didn't give a damn what anyone thought.

And then he realized that he had always been
telling himself that, and that maybe now, for the first
time in his life, it was the truth.

In a little while the prisoners were fed. A machine
brought in a big cake of mottled pink and green stuff,
the same tasteless substance Gil had lived on since
his capture eight or ten days ago. While he ate he sat
off to one side by himself, looking at nothing and
listening to the two sharp guys talking to each other
in low voices.

Rom was saying: "Look—we're in what was the
crew quarters, right?"

"If you say so."

"Right. Now they brought me in through the forward compartment, the control room, and I had a
chance to take a quick look around there. And I've
paced off the length of this chamber we're in. I tell
you I served aboard one of these ships for a year; I
know 'em inside out."

"So?"

"Just this—" There came a faint scrape and shudder through the hull. When Rom spoke again his low voice was charged with excitement. "Feel that? We're going spaceborne again, the big machine's sending this ship somewhere, for some reason. That means we would have a chance, if only . . . Listen, the circuitry that makes up the brain that's controlling this ship and keeping us prisoner, *has* to be spread out along that plastic bulkhead at the forward end of this compartment we're in. On the control room side there's another plastic slab been installed, and the circuitry must be sandwiched in between the two."

"How can you know?" Hudak sounded skeptical.

Rom's voice dropped even lower, giving arguments most of which Gil could not hear. ". . . as well protected there against outside attack as anywhere in the ship . . . paced off the distance . . . overhead here, look at the modifications in the power conduits going forward . . ."

Hudak: "You're right, I guess. Or at least it seems probable. That plastic barrier is all that keeps us from getting at it, then. I wonder how thick . . ."

Gil could see from the corner of his eye that the two sharp guys were trying not to look at what they were talking about; but he was free to stare. The forward end of the big chamber they were in was a blank greenish plastic wall, pierced along the top for some pipes, and at one side by the door through which Gil had been brought in.

"Thick enough, of course. We don't have so much as a screwdriver, and we'd probably need a cutting torch or a hydraulic jack—"

Hudak nudged Rom and they fell silent. The door

forward had opened, and one of the man-sized machines came in.

"Gilberto Klee," it twanged. "Come."

Rom had been right, they were spaceborne again, away from the big berserker. In the forward compartment Gil had a moment to look out before the man-sized machine turned him away from a view of stars and faced him toward a squat console, a thing of eye-like lights and a radio-like speaker, which seemed to crouch before the front of the plastic wall.

"Gilberto Klee," said the console's speaker. "It is my purpose to keep a number of human life-units alive and in good health."

For a while, Gil thought.

The speaker said: "The standard nutrient on which prisoners are fed is evidently lacking in one or more necessary trace ingredients. In several places where prisoners are being held symptoms of nutritional deficiency have developed, including general debility, loss of sight, loss of teeth." Pause. "Are you aware of my meaning?"

"Yeah, I just don't talk much."

"You, Gilberto Klee, are experienced at growing life-forms to be consumed by human life-units as food. You will begin here in this ship to grow food for yourself and other human life-units."

There was a pause that stretched on. Gil could see the Old Man very plainly, and hear him scream.

"Squash would be good," Gil said at last. "I know how to raise it, and there's lots of vitamins and stuff in the kind of squash we had at the Station. But I'd need seeds, and soil . . ."

"A quantity of soil has been provided," said the console. And the man-sized machine picked up and held open a plastic case that was divided into many compartments. "And seeds," the console added. "Which are the ones for squash?"

When Gil was returned to the prison chamber other machines were already busy there with the modifications he had said would be needed. They were adding more overhead lights, and covering most of the deck space with wide, deep trays. These trays were set on the transverse girders of the inner hull revealed by the removal of decking. Under the trays drainage pipes were being connected, while sprinklers went high overhead. Into the trays the machines were dumping soil they carted from somewhere in the rear of the ship.

Gil gave his fellow prisoners an explanation of what was going on.

"So that's why it took you and some of the other farmers alive," said Hudak. "There must be a lot of different places where human prisoners are being held and maybe bred for experiments. Lots of healthy animals needed."

"So," said Rom, looking sideways at Gil. "You're going to do what it wants?"

"A guy has to keep himself alive," Gil said, "before he can do anything else."

Rom began in a heated whisper: "Is it better that a berserker's prisoners should be kept—" But he broke off when one of the man-sized machines paused nearby, as if it was watching and listening.

They came to call that machine the Overseer, because from then on it never left the humans, though the other machines departed when the construction job was done. Through the Overseer the berserker-brain controlling the ship informed Gil that the other

prisoners were there mainly as a labor pool should
he need human help in food-growing. Gil thought it
over briefly. "I don't need no help—yet. Just leave
the people stay here for now, but I'll do the planting."

Spacing the hills and dropping the seeds was easy
enough, though the machines had left no aisles between the trays of soil except a small passage leading
to the door. The trays furthest forward almost touched
the plastic bulkhead, and others were laid edge to
edge back to within a few paces of the rear. The
machines gave Gil a platform the size of a short
surfboard, on which he could sit or lie while hovering at a steady two feet above the soil. Hudak said
the thing must work by a kind of hole in the artificial
gravity field. On the platform was a simple control
lever by means of which Gil could cause it to move
left or right, forward or back. Almost as soon as the
planting was done, he had to start tending his fast-
growing vines. The vines had to be twisted to make
them grow along the soil in the proper direction, and
then there were extra blossoms to be pinched off. A
couple of the other prisoners offered to help, despite
Rom's scowling at them, but Gil refused the offer.
You had to have a knack, he said, and some training,
and he did it all himself.

The two sharp guys had little to say to Gil about
anything anymore, but they were plainly interested
in his surfboard; one day while the Overseer's back
was turned Rom took Gil hurriedly aside. Rom whispered quickly and feverishly, like a man taking what
he knows is a crazy chance, fed up enough to take it
anyway. "The Overseer doesn't pay much attention
to you anymore when you're working, Gil. You could
take that platform of yours—" Rom's right hand,
extended horizontally, rammed the tips of its fingers

into the palm of his vertical left hand. "—into the wall. If you could only make a little crack in the plastic, a hole big enough to stick a hand through— we'd have some kind of chance—I'd do it but the Overseer won't let anyone but you near the platform."

Gil's lip curled. "*I* ain't gonna try nothin' like that."

The thin sickly man was not used to snotty kids talking back to him, and he flared feebly into anger. "You think the berserker's going to take good care of *you?*"

"The machine built the platform, didn't it?" Gil demanded. "Wouldn't give us nothing we could bust through there with. Not if there's anything so important as you think back there."

For a moment Gil thought Rom was going to swing at him, but other people held Rom back. And suddenly the Overseer was no longer standing on the other side of the chamber with its back turned, but right in front of Rom, staring at him with its lenses. A few long, long seconds passed before it was plain that the machine was not going to do anything this time. But maybe its hearing was better than the sharp guys had thought.

"They ain't ripe yet, but we can eat some of 'em anyway," said Gil a couple of weeks later as he slid off his platform to join the other people in the few square yards of living space left along the chamber's rear bulkhead. Cradled in Gil's arm were half a dozen dull yellowish ovoids. He turned casually to the Overseer and asked: "Got a knife?"

There was a pause. Then the Overseer extended a hand, from which a wicked blade extended itself like

an extra finger. "I will divide the fruit," it said, and
proceeded to do so with great precision.

The little group of prisoners had come crowding
around, some interest stirring in their dull eyes.
They ate greedily the little morsels that the Overseer
doled out; anything tasted good after weeks or months
of nothing but the changeless pink-and-green cake.
Rom, after a scarcely perceptible hesitation, joined
the others in eating some raw squash. He showed no
enjoyment as the others did. It was just that a man
had to be healthy, he seemed to be thinking, before
he could persuade others to get themselves killed, or
let themselves sicken and die.

Under the optimum conditions provided by the
berserker at Gil's direction, only weeks rather than
months were needed for the trays to become filled
with broad roundish leaves, spreading above a profusion of thickening, ground-hugging vines. Half of the
fast-growing fruit were hidden under leaves, while
others burgeoned in the full light, and a few hung
over the edges of the trays, resting their new weight
on the girders under the trays or sagging all the way
to the deck.

Gil maintained that the time for a proper harvest
was still an indefinite number of days away. But each
day he now came back to the living area with a single
squash to be divided by the Overseer's knife; and
each day the fruit he brought was larger.

He was out in the middle of his "fields," lying
prone on his platform and staring moodily at a swell-
ing squash, when the sound of a sudden commotion
back in the living area made him raise himself and
turn his head.

The center of the commotion was the Overseer.

The machine was hopping into the air again and again, as if the brain that controlled it had gone berserker indeed. The prisoners cried out, scrambling to get away from the Overseer. Then the machine stopped its mad jumping, and stood turning in a slow circle, shivering, the knife-finger on its hand flicking in and out repeatedly.

"Attention, we are entering battle," the Overseer proclaimed suddenly, dead monotone turned up to deafening volume. "Under attack. All prisoners are to be—they will all—"

It said more, but at a speed no human ear could follow, gibbering up the frequency scale to end in something like a human scream. The mad girl who never spoke let out a blending yell of terror.

The Overseer tottered and swayed, brandishing its knife. It babbled and twitched—like an old man with steel fingers vising his head. Then it leaned forward, leaned further, and fell on its face, disappearing from Gil's sight below the level of trays and vines, striking the deck with a loud clang.

That clang was echoed, forward, by a cannon-crack of sound. Gil had been keeping himself from looking in that direction, but now he turned. The plastic wall had been split across the center third of its extent by a horizontal fissure a few feet above the trays.

Gil lay still on his platform, watching cautiously. Ensign Rom came charging across the trays and past him, trampling the crop unheedingly, to hurl himself at the wall. Even cracked, it resisted his onslaught easily, but he kept pounding at it with his fists, trying to force his fingers into the tiny crevice. Gil looked back the other way. The Overseer was still down. Hudak was trying the forward door and finding it locked. Then he, followed by the others, scrambled over trays to help Rom.

Gil tested his platform's control and found that it no longer worked, though the platform was still aloft. He got up from it, setting foot in soil for the first time in a couple of months; it was a good feeling. Then he lifted the thin metal platform sideways out of its null and carried it over to where everyone else was already struggling with the wall. "Here," Gil said, "try sticking the corner of this in the crack and pryin'."

It took them several hours of steady effort to make a hole in the wall big enough for Rom to squeeze through. In a minute he was back, crying and shouting, announcing freedom and victory. They were in control of the ship!

When he came back the second time, he was in control of himself as well, and puzzled. "What cracked the wall, though? There's no fighting, no other ships around—"

He fell silent as he joined Hudak in staring down into the narrow space between the furthest forward tray and the slightly bulged-in section of wall where the strain had come to force the first crack above. Gil had already looked down there into the niches between wall and transverse girder. Those niches were opened up now, displaying their contents—the dull yellowish fruit Gil had guided into place with a pinch and a twist of vine. The fruit had been very small then, but now they were huge, and cracked gently open with the sudden release of their own internal pressure.

Funny pulpy things that a man could break with a kick, or a steel hand squeeze through like nothing

. . . "But growth is stubborn, boys," the Old Man said, squinting to read a dial, then piling more weights onto the machine with the growing squash inside it, a machine he'd set up to catch kids' eyes and minds. "Can't take a sudden shock. Slow. But now, look. Five thousand pounds pressure per square inch. All from millions of tiny cells, just growing, all together. Ever see a tree root swell under a concrete walk—?"

It was on Rom's and Hudak's faces now that they understood. Gil nodded to them once and smiled just faintly to make sure they knew it had been no accident. Then the smile faded from his face as he looked up at the edges of broken plastic, the shattered tracery of what had been a million sandwiched printed circuits.

"I hope it was slow," Gil said. "I hope it felt the whole thing."

A truth can be a potent weapon. So can a lie. I touched a scrupulous and honest mind, that lied to enforce honesty . . .

THE ANNIHILATION OF ANGKOR APEIRON

The battle was a long one for deep space, lasting well over a standard hour, and as fierce as any fight in which the losing side can have no expectation of survival. Commander Ridolfi had fought his heavy cruiser, the *Dipavamsa*, with a desperate skill that twice in a matter of minutes forestalled instant destruction by the berserker's missiles, and each member of his crew performed superbly well in making such combat decisions as could be handled slowly enough to let human brains cooperate with their slave computers.

The human crew of course faced death or worse if they should lose. And the berserker, their unliving foe, faced its own analogue of death and worse-than-death. To lose would mean destruction—which was nothing to a berserker if destruction could bring victory. But destruction in defeat meant certain failure to achieve any further progress toward its programmed goal, the annihilation of all life, whenever and wherever it could be attacked.

Aboard the *Dipavamsa* there were only four civilian passengers, including Otto Novotny, who in his

37

long life had never come close to taking part in a battle before and who felt a great deal too old and paunchy for such endeavors now. Nevertheless he was more alert than any of the other civilians, and had begun to don his requisite suit of space armor as soon as the Battle Stations klaxon sounded, while the other three were still wondering aloud if it was only practice.

Ten seconds later the first berserker missile blew against the cruiser's defensive screens, a mere kilometer from her hull, and they all knew better.

Dipavamsa was fighting for her life several light years from any star, along a trade route where in these last few standard months no unarmed vessels had dared to try to pass. The berserker machine, a sphere some forty or fifty kilometers in diameter, all armor and combat computers and heavy weapons and drive, had waited like a spider in the midst of the net of detectors it had planted in subspace. The region where its detectors existed was conterminous to one in normal space where a strait of hard vacuum bent between two nebulae, forming a bottleneck only a few billion kilometers wide in which a reasonably fast passage could be achieved. When a manned ship dared to try the strait—heavy cruiser or not—the berserker jumped to the attack.

Locked together with their armaments of fields and counterfields like grappling ocean ships of old, the contending metallic giants rolled into normal space, there to remain until the issue was decided. After the first enemy missile-blast reverberated through the cruiser's hull, Novotny thought that the battle would probably be over one way or the other before he could get himself completely into the unfamiliar armor. His efforts were complicated by a sudden lack of artificial gravity; every erg of the cruiser's energies was suddenly needed for more important things than maintaining a rightsideup.

But he persevered, working with the same methodical speed with which he usually solved problems of quite a different kind, and finally got the armor on. No sooner had he sealed its last seam and begun to wonder what to do next, when *Dipavamsa's* hull was breached by blast and beam. Hatches slammed to seal compartments, but the air in their compartment could not be held and Novotny saw the lives of his companions who had been too slow snuffed out like candle flames.

After that the battle became a scrambling confusion of largely physical effort for the humans who took part in it. For Novotny especially, who had less idea of what to expect than did any of the cruiser's crew and who was not in as good shape as they were either. Now the berserker chose to hurl some of its auxiliary machines across the narrow no-man's-land of space to try to board the cruiser. It could use the ship if it could capture it still reasonably intact, and probably it wanted living prisoners.

Prisoners of course were useful for interrogation, after which a berserker generally killed them quickly; it was programmed only to pursue death, not suffering, though of course it was quite willing to apply judicious torture to extract information of value in advancing the cause of death. And prisoners were needed for experiments that the berserkers carried on extensively, in an effort to learn what made Homo Sapiens, a species now spread across this part of the

Galaxy, such a resistant life-form to their relentless program of sterilization.

The berserkers were automated warships, made by an unknown race to fight in an interstellar war that had been over ages since; they had outlasted their original enemies and their makers as well, having been programmed and equipped to rebuild and reproduce themselves. Still trying to carry out their originally programmed task, they had made an age-long progress across the spiral arms, leaving nothing living in their wake.

While following the motions of the Commander's arms, which were gesturing to shovel suited people from one wrecked-looking compartment to another, Novotny had a chance to look out through the holed hull to catch his first glimpse of the enemy. The monstrous spherical hull of the berserker was visible by the cherry-glow of craters that the cruiser's weapons had pocked across its armor hide. One crater flared anew while Novotny watched, flamed with some power that seemed to be eating like a cancer into the enemy's metal bowels. But again the cruiser was rocked and shaken in its turn. Novotny and Commander Ridolfi were picked up by the same invisible hand and slammed together into a bulkhead, saved only by their suits from broken bones.

Now some of the berserker's boarding machines, which were a little bigger than men and of diverse shapes, managed to get aboard *Dipavamsa*, and Novotny had a chance to see the enemy at close range. Men, some of whom were hardened veterans, were screaming around him in terror, but his own unconsciously-maintained attitude was that under conditions like these one could hardly spare the time to be frightened. Vaguely he thought of this situation as resembling an impossible editorial deadline—one thing that could never help was panic. He followed as best he could the Commander's waved and shouted orders, and kept alert. At last he got his own chance to blaze away at the foe, with a small recoilless rifle he had snatched up from a fallen crewman's hands.

By that time—as Novotny confusedly understood, from scraps of combat jargon that came into his helmet—Commander Ridolfi had ordered his Second Officer and a picked crew to leave the cruiser in an armed launch that could take shelter among the drifts and waves of nebular material in space nearby, darting through where the bulky berserker could not pass at speed. It was a feigned acknowledgement of defeat, intended to make the enemy think they were abandoning ship, a battle tactic to lure the damaged enemy in where a sharp counterattack might still destroy it.

Ridolfi himself, as the cruiser's commanding officer, and Novotny, as more or less useless baggage, were among those who stayed aboard her and tried to fight a delaying action through her corridors. The vacuum around Novotny's helmet continued to buzz and sing with the strange energies of this battle; he clutched his recoilless rifle and continued to fire it toward the enemy's boarding machines whenever he caught a glimpse of one of them. He could not have said whether or not his shots were doing any good. He also tried to stay close to Ridolfi's side; whether he felt in slighly less hopeless danger there, or was hoping thus to improve his chances of being useful, he did not pause to consider. Ridolfi indeed kept snapping orders, but they were meant for members of his crew.

The two of them were still together, trying to

defend the central control room of the ship, when
Death struck closer to them than at any moment yet.

It came very suddenly. One moment Novotny was
still looking toward Ridolfi for a hint of what they
might try to do next—and the next moment a berserker machine that looked like a cross between a
centipede and a crab had thrown itself upon them
and they were prisoners. Steel claws that moved
with the force of atomic power effortlessly tore
Novotny's rocket launcher away and wrenched the
Commander's sidearm from his hand. The berserker
shifted its grip then, holding each pair of human
arms helpless with a single claw—and then machine
and men went down together in a tangle as a new
force slammed at the cruiser from outside. The Second Officer and his picked crew, in their fresh and
undamaged launch, had begun their counterattack.

The crab-centipede was wrecked, sheared almost
in two, as the launch sent something like the Angel
of the Lord passing almost invisibly through the embattled ship, cutting selectively, passing over fragile
human bodies and machinery that it could somehow
identify as human property.

The mass of his late captor, and its tenacious grip
which had not relaxed with the destruction of its
computer-brain, pinned Novotny in an angle between
deck and bulkhead, surrounded by wreckage. Beside
him Ridolfi grunted and struggled in similar difficul-
ties. Then they abruptly ceased their efforts to get
free, simultaneously ceased even to breathe—another
berserker machine was entering the damaged control
room.

If it was aware of them, it did not turn. It moved
straight to one of the panels before which a human
astrogator normally sat, and with a startling delicacy

began to remove the panel from its mounting. Neatly—almost timidly, it seemed—it probed for the panel fasteners, teasing and tickling at them with grasping devices that could have ripped the panel free like so much tissue paper.

. . . it was working so carefully, and now it almost had what it was after. It reached inside and pulled out . . . very slowly . . .

. . . a small metal case . . .

That burst into a flaming snowball even as the berserker oh so gently tugged it free of its connections, a blaze that here in free fall sent out its flames in a sunburst of straight radii, a wad of radiant glory that the enemy instantly hurled away. Without pause the enemy turned to snatch up a small bundle of paper printout that writhed weightlessly across the deck. It shoved this inside itself, door slamming shut protectively across the orifice—and the machine was gone, lunging with inhuman speed out of the room again.

"Novotny." The two of them gasped for breath again and once more struggled against the dead claws that held them prisoner. "Look—can you shift your weight this way? Lean on it here, maybe I can get a hand out of this claw . . ."

After a minute or two of cooperative effort both of them were free. From some comparatively great distance the shocks and slams of battle were still coming to them through the hull. "Novotny, listen to me." The Commander talked while looking for his pistol, which he at last grabbed from a turning swirl of other weightless debris that drifted in the middle of the room. "It was going after our astrogational databank just then. After that thing that burst into flame?"

"I saw."

"It didn't get what it wanted, because the bank's destructor charge worked when it was pulled out. But it must need astrogational information badly, or it wouldn't have sent a machine after it, before the battle's even over. Maybe its own banks have been shot up."

Novotny moved his head inside his helmet, showing that he understood so far.

The Commander had his pistol back, held absently in his right hand, and his left hand clamped briefly on Novotny's suited arm. "I believe you have in your quarters something it could use as a substitute. I understand you're traveling with the whole new edition of Encyclopedia Galactica in microstorage—and the EG gives galactic coordinates for all inhabited systems, right?"

Novotny agreed again. Now that he had been almost immobile for a little while, his muscles were starting to stiffen from the unaccustomed workout. He could hear the wheezings from inside his own chest, and his body was beginning to feel like so much fluid lead. If they weren't in free fall he would certainly be dizzy and have to sit down. Decades at a senior executive's desk had left him too fat and old for this kind of nonsense.

But he was moving again now, keeping up with the agile Commander as they picked their way out of the ruined control room, which now looked not in fit shape for controlling anything.

"Then we've got to get to your quarters," the Commander was saying, "while there's still a chance. You've got just the one copy of the encyclopedia there?"

"Yes."

"We must see that it's destroyed."

They had started down a corridor, and there came a glimpse of a machine moving ahead of them, and the vibrations of its massy passage came through the bulkheads to their gripping hands. Taking shelter together in a doorway, they waited for it to get out of their way.

The Commander kept trying to make contact with his Second Officer by suit radio, but seemed unable to get any reply. Maybe, thought Novotny, it's only that the space between is far too noisy . . .

"Commander," he asked, when there was a momentary opportunity, "What sector are we in now? Of the Galaxy, I mean, in Revised Galactic Coordinates?"

Ridolfi's eyes came to full focus on him for what might have been the first time. "Omicron Sector, Ring Eleven—what does it matter? Oh, you mean you want to know which volumes of your set it will be most important to destroy. Good thinking. That damned machine will be too shot up itself to get out of Omicron without help. I don't think it'll be able to catch another ship, even if one should come along. It'll be trying to find an undefended planet nearby, within a light year or two if possible, preferably an inhabited one where there'll be machines it can take over and some ready-made materials that it can use to repair itself."

"And my encyclopedia is now the only means by which it can locate such a planet?"

"That's the way I read the situation. It can't just go visiting stars at random, the chance of success is far too small . . . remember that printout it picked up from the control room floor? That was a copy of what we call the Military Information Sheet, which we got when we filed our flight plan. Among other things it contains a list of all the *defended* planets along our projected course—all the places where we might be able to look for help in case of an emergency. I suppose it'll go for one of them if it can't find anything better. But in your reference book it's likely to get the address of some undefended one . . . the war's a recent thing in this neck of the galactic woods, remember?"

Novotny's face bore a doubtful look, but the Commander was no longer watching him.

"Coast's clear, Novotny. Let's move." Then the two of them were in motion again, diving and scrambling in free fall. For the moment their luck held; no more berserkers came in sight as they reached the stateroom corridor and swam along it to the door of Novotny's cabin. The door had been jammed shut by some warping of the battered ship around it, and it took the men an agonizing moment or two to force it free.

Then they were inside. "Where is it?"

"There on the table, Commander. Already plugged into the reading machine. But wait." A new anxiety had come into Novotny's voice. "I'm not sure that destruction is our wisest move."

Commander Ridolfi only looked at him. "Get back."

But Novotny had not moved when a third figure suddenly joined them in the little cabin; the crab-centipede's cousin, which raised a multitude of claws.

The Commander aimed his gun again, but not at the berserker. He thought his own life and battle now lost anyway, and more important than perhaps damaging one more of the berserker's machines would be denying it this information on new targets. He aimed at the reading machine that sat like some dull sculpture on the table.

Novotny reached out deliberately and knocked Ridolfi's arm aside.

The berserker, on the verge of killing both of them, hesitated fractionally as it observed their struggle. Did one of these life-units wish to become goodlife, a willing ally of the cause of Death? Such conversions had happened before, more than a few times, and a goodlife could be very useful. And what on the table was so important that a life-unit struggled to destroy it—?

From the armed launch came the next phase of counterattack. The cabin was nearly ripped apart. The berserker lashed out at Ridolfi, and the Commander saw that his pistol was gone again, before it could be fired, and his arm gone with it almost to the shoulder. The suit will seal itself around the wound, he thought, in sudden massive shock that made all things seem trivial. He saw the reading machine snatched up from the table in the claws of the berserker, and the launch's weapons struck again. A fresh gust of escaping atmosphere whirled through the cruiser from a newly-ruptured compartment, and with the last glow of his consciousness the Commander could see stars.

His first feeling when his wits came back was sheer astonishment at being still alive. Astonishment deepened when he realized that he had somehow been brought on board the armored launch. All four bunks in its tiny sick bay were full of wounded, and men and women and machines were steadily at work, passing back and forth continually in the small space between the bunks.

The Second Officer came in to report, relief dawning on his face when he saw that Ridolfi was getting up and evidently in shape to resume his command. Shock and loss of blood had been treated, pain blocked, and bandages sealed the wound from which a new arm could one day be made to grow.

The Second made his report concisely. The launch was now some half a million kilometers within the nebula, its defenses alertly repelling or safely detonating—so far—all the torpedoes that the berserker had sent after it. The battle had ground to a halt, otherwise, in mutual though incomplete destruction. What was left of the cruiser had now been abandoned by both contending forces. Before pulling back deep within the nebula, the launch had dared to delay long enough to follow distress signals and pick up two suited survivors who had, it seemed, somehow been blown clean away from the embattled cruiser in the last stages of the fighting. One of the survivors was Commander Ridolfi himself. The other . . .

"That makes nineteen people on the air and food," the Second Officer mused, as they stood looking down at the collapsed shape of Otto Novotny, slumped in total exhaustion in a corner of the small dayroom where there hardly seemed room for his gross form. "Still, we should be able to recycle, and make supplies last until we're eventually picked up . . ."

"I don't know if there'll be nineteen or not, for very long." Ridolfi's voice was hard as that of one just going into battle, not coming out of it, and his eyes were welded on the fat civilian.

"Sir?" The Second didn't get it at all, not yet.

"I mean, Mister, that unless I get some questions answered by this man here, and answered damn fast, I'm going to convene a formal court and press charges against him of voluntarily aiding a berserker."

*   *   *

There were only six people in the dayroom when the first informal inquiry began; the Commander didn't want to prejudice possible jurors if the thing came to a formal trial, which he was empowered to give even civilians when in space and in the face of the enemy.

As Novotny, by now somewhat recovered though still slow of movement and blinking a bit bewilderedly, was ushered in and shown to the seat across the table from him, the Commander was simultaneously handed a note from the other side. It informed him that the berserker had just been observed dropping out of normal space in the area of the battle. Instruments showed it departing the local area, having evidently completed such emergency repairs as it could manage on the spot. A reading on the subspace signals of its departure gave a vector for its probable destination that deepened the lines carved down through Ridolfi's cheeks.

A silence grew in the room, until Ridolfi spoke. "This is not yet a trial, Mr. Novotny. But I warn you that there may be one before we get back to a planet, if we ever do; or are picked up by another human ship, if we ever are. If there is a trial, you will be charged with voluntarily aiding a berserker, and conviction will carry an almost certain penalty of death."

Exhaustion and puzzlement seemed to be absorbed almost at once within the layers of fat as Novotny pulled himself together. "Ah. I stand ready, of course, Commander, to answer any questions on my behavior that you may have."

"That's good. Frank answers will be required." Ridolfi tried to keep his one hand from fidgeting before him on the table. "On board the cruiser, in a

combat situation, you deliberately interfered with
my attempt to destroy the databank containing your
encyclopedia. Do you deny it?"

Novotny was sitting very still, as if he feared that
movement might land him in further trouble of some
kind. He thought before answering, and his face
maintained a frown. "No, I do not deny that,
Commander."

The Commander paused, then put his arm out on
the table, fingers opened, elbow straight, a dominat-
ing gesture. "You do not. Very well. My intention in
destroying that data, sir, was to prevent its use as an
astrogational aid by the berserker. If you wanted to
save it, it was surely not for yourself. Did you expect
that the berserker might accord you some favorable
treatment if you . . ."

Novotny was shaking his head. "I very seriously
doubt that the data in the encyclopedia will do the
enemy the least bit of good, in this case. Nor did I
wish to help the enemy."

The Commander's voice was relentlessly unchanged.
"On the cruiser, you and I both saw the berserker
going after the astrogational databank, which it evidently needed but didn't get.

"We also know the enemy is severely damaged,
which means it will be looking for some comparatively near planet where it can commandeer machinery and materials to repair itself; in addition, of
course, to wiping out as many unprotected human
lives there as it can reach. Because we fought it to a
standstill here in space doesn't mean it won't be able
to poison an atmosphere and depopulate a planet, if
it comes on one only lightly defended or takes one
unaware. Is all this news to you?"

"I think I understand all this, Commander."

"Let those who are here with us be witness that you do." Ridolfi glanced briefly round at the faces of the others, all of them staring now at the accused. "Because so far you are answering yourself right into a trial, Mister Novotny. There are only two things, basically, that a berserker ever wants or needs: victims, and facilities for repair and refitting. And you've shown this one where to go for both of them."

Novotny slumped a little in his chair and closed his eyes. But when he opened them his voice was as steady as before. "Commander, if I am indeed on trial for my life, or likely to be, then I would like to hear the charges and the evidence as fully as possible before I try to answer them. Go on."

"Very well." Ridolfi nodded grimly. "You came on board the *Dipavamsa* with two copies of your new edition, one of which was subsequently and routinely stowed aboard this launch, along with some other baggage not immediately in use. That copy is still here and available, and since going off combat alert I've fed it into our computer and asked for a readout —as the berserker can readily do with the copy you gave it—of all inhabited planets within seven light years of where our battle was fought. That's about as far as that berserker is going to get without repairs; and extending the radius another light year or so brings no new planets in."

The Commander had a paper which he now consulted. "There are seven inhabited planets to be found, according to the Encyclopedia Galactica, within that radius. They are Angkor Apeiron, Comparettia, Epirus, Francavilla, Han Kao, Reissner, and Yang Ch'i. Exact coordinates, RGC, are given for each." He put one piece of paper on the table and took another from a pocket of his shirt. "I have here part of a spare copy of the Military Information Sheet given us when we filed our flight plan before departing on this trip. Among other things, it lists the six inhabited planets in this same region that have notable ground defenses, or fleet units standing by, or both. As one more bit of evidence, Mr. Novotny, let me state now that you were also a witness with me that a copy of this list of the six defended planets was also seized by the berserker. Any denials yet?" Ridolfi's fingers were shaking and he put the second paper down.

"Not yet, Commander."

"Though whether you understood the full implications of that seizure at the time . . ."

"I had . . . some idea, I suppose, of what the implications were. Proceed."

Ridolfi read: "The six defended planets on the military list for this region are: Comparettia, Epirus, Francavilla, Han Kao, Reissner, and Yang Ch'i. Notably missing from this military list is Angkor Apeiron." The Commander pushed his second paper out on the table beside the first, where anyone who wished might look them over, and then produced a third.

He went on: "According to the latest census figures, as given in this EG article, this world has about eleven million, six hundred thousand inhabitants. Its chief export industries are crystal growing and natural honey. The spaceport is small, but probably the berserker could plunder it for useful machines and materials after it has wiped out what appears to be an undefended populace.

The Commander needed a moment before he could continue. "Angkor Apeiron was discovered by Chang Izanagi, of Hathor, in 7626 CE . . . first colonized only ten standard years later." His voice was starting to shake a little like his hand. "I suppose your reference work is quite reliable in these particulars? I mean, about there being eleven million people there, especially?"

Novotny paused for thought, began to speak, then stopped and shook his head and tried again. "The EG is the most reliable general reference work in human history, Your Honor—Commander—whatever I am to call you now—"

" 'Commander' will still do."

"—when it is used for the purposes for which it is intended. Which is to say that it was never meant to serve as a manual of do-it-yourself medicine, or law, or astrogation either. It is a means by which one can verify, or learn, a fact; check a date or name; obtain entree to almost any field of knowledge, and learn where to go for further . . ."

"Yes. Spare us the sales talk, we're not in the market for a set right now." Nobody cracked a smile. "Now here in your reliable reference work, which you gave the enemy as a present, are the precise coordinates for the Apeiron system: Sector Omicron 111.254, Ring Eleven 87.58, Galactic Latitude 7.54 North. These figures are correct, are they not? Hasn't the EG a competent editorial staff, with the technical and scientific knowledge . . ."

"The staff at the home office is more than competent, Commander. It is very good indeed. I speak from personal experience."

The Commander leaned forward. "Then what, Mr. Novotny, is going to save the inhabitants of Angkor Apeiron from the consequences of your action?"

Novotny leaned back, somewhat haughtily, as if he had at last taken affront. "Only the fact, Commander, that the inhabitants of Angkor Apeiron do not exist."

There was a silence in the dayroom, as if each
person who looked at the speaker were waiting for
his last words to somehow clear themselves out of
the air, or for some great hand to reach in from
outside the little ship and mend the broken spring of
sanity.

The Commander, his shakiness shocked away, was
the first to reply: "You mean . . . you claim to have
some knowledge . . . that the planet has already
been evacuated, or wiped out?"

"I mean, sir, that the star Apeiron has no planets.
It has never had any. When the berserker arrives
there it will find no victims and no material help; and
if your estimate of its damaged condition is as accurate as I would like to believe, before it can go on to
some other world it will have died, if that is the
proper word, of the injuries your crew has so gallantly
inflicted on it."

"But . . ." The Second Officer was starting a dis-
believing protest.

Novotny rounded on him sharply. "Why do you
suppose the military authorities protected six settled
planets in this region and ignored a seventh?"

"Lack sufficient forces . . ."

"Bah. Correct me if I am wrong, Commander, but
would not the general or admiral in charge be more
likely to spread his forces thinner, and not leave
eleven million people totally undefended, since this
sector has become a combat zone? Of course his
forces are probably spread all too thin already, which
is why I thought it good to direct our late antagonist
to a desert system, rather than letting it go challenge
some of them."

Ridolfi had recovered, or almost. "Desert system?

But this EG entry . . . you claim your encyclopedia is the most reliable . . ."

Novotny was holding up a pudgy, magisterial hand, and his face had eased into something that approached a smile. "I will explain, as I have promised. But to do so I must briefly go far afield from berserkers and space warfare."

His accuser had not yet relaxed a bit. "Do so. Go as far as you like. But be sure that you come back."

Novotny took another moment to marshall his thoughts before he spoke. "Suppose . . . suppose that you, Commander, are a ruthlessly good businessman, back on Earth or one of the other crowded worlds. And you decide that there is money to be made in purveying information to the public, even as EG makes money. You decide that you will compile and sell a general reference work. Or perhaps one more specialized—on galactography, let us say, listing and describing all the inhabited and explored planets as well as other bodies in the Galaxy that are for some reason interesting.

"You decide that you will put a great deal less work into your encyclopedia than we put into ours, and therefore be able to sell yours for a great deal less money, while including the same information we include. How? The most direct expedient is of course to copy all your articles verbatim from ours; but this the laws and courts, alas for your enterprise, are never going to allow. You are forced to the inconvenience of at least rewriting our material somewhat as you crib.

"Given a little computer help, to rearrange the syntax and replace words with their synonyms, this will not be such an arduous task as might at first appear. Even our several billions of words might be rehashed and reprinted, in slightly different format, in a quite reasonable time. Behold! And Commander Ridolfi's Encyclopedia of All Knowledge is available for the home databank, at a much lower fee than ours . . . never mind that you will not provide your customers with the constant updating service that ours receive.

"So! Even with much rewriting, your basic idea is still illegal, still infringes upon our copyrights, does it not? Well, now the answer is no longer quite so clear-cut. But believe me, our lawyers will try, *have* tried in similar cases, to sue you for a bundle, as soon as they find out what you have done.

"Now you show up for trial, and are on the witness stand, though not with your life at stake of course . . . Commander Ridolfi, I the prosecuting attorney ask you: Is it true or not, that you have compiled your so-called reference work virtually entirely from EG? Now think carefully, for on your answer your whole defense will stand or fall.

"Of course it is not true! you answer ringingly. You used the Merchant Astrogation banks, you used periodicals and the records from dusty archives, you looked in books, you queried eminent authorities in many fields, just as does the great EG itself.

"Ohh? I ask, and now my voice is of the softest, and I cast an eye toward the jury. Then tell me, sir, which of these many indispensable sources did you use to cross-check your information on the planet Angkor Apeiron?"

There was another silence in the dayroom, a different sort of silence this time, and death that had all along seemed close was suddenly light years off again, at one with the berserker's wake that faded in subspace.

Novotny felt the difference and began to sag. "Because you see, sir, we have made this entry up, population, industries, discovery date and all, as encyclopedists have made up entries for the same reason from very ancient times. We made it up to catch such plagiaristic fish as you, and put it as bait for you within the great EG, and nowhere else in the great universe of worlds or information storage does Angkor Apeiron exist . . . there are a number of other baits like this one, Commander, among our forty million entries. Quite a few, like this one, I had a hand in making up myself; but how many there are altogether I do not know; no one man or woman knows them all. The ordinary user is of course never going to hear of Angkor Apeiron anywhere and is therefore never going to look it up. If he comes upon it while browsing at his reading machine, he is only treated to a dull and minor fantasy that he will soon forget."

Novotny let himself sink back into a chair that no longer seemed to be a dock above the edge of death. Then he turned his head to a wallscreen showing space, and looked off into the nebular cloudbanks of the Deep. "I wonder if it can even *wonder* how it was tricked, or how it tricked itself . . . I know that it could never understand."

*There are times when no weapon less strong and direct
than the truth will serve. But, to use the truth, one first
must find it out.*

INHUMAN ERROR

When the dreadnought *Hamilcar Barca* came out
of the inhuman world of plus-space into the blue-
white glare of Meitner's Sun the forty men and women
of the dreadnought's crew were taut at their battle
stations, not knowing whether or not the whole berserker fleet would be around them as they emerged.
But then they were in normal space, seconds of time
were ticking calmly by, and there were only the stars
and galaxies to be seen, no implacable, inanimate
killers coming to the attack. The tautness eased a
little.

Captain Liao, his lean frame strapped firmly into
the combat chair in the center of the dreadnought's
bridge, had brought his ship back into normal space
as close to Meitner's Sun as he dared—operating on
interstellar, *c*-plus drive in a gravitational field this
strong was dangerous, to put it mildly—but the orbit
of the one planet of the system worth being concerned about was still tens of millions of kilometers
closer to the central sun. It was known simply as
Meitner's Planet, and was the one rock in the system
habitable in terms of gravity and temperature.

Before his ship had been ten standard seconds in
normal space, Liao had begun to focus a remote-

controlled telescope to bring the planet into close
view on a screen that hung before him on the bridge.
Luck had brought him to the same side of the sun
that the planet happened to be on; it showed under
magnification on the screen as a thin illuminated
crescent, covered with fluffy-looking perpetual clouds.
Somewhere beneath those clouds a human colony of
about ten thousand people dwelt, for the most part
under the shelter of one huge ceramic dome. The
colonists had begun work on the titanic project of
converting the planet's ammonia atmosphere to a
breathable one of nitrogen and oxygen. Meanwhile
they held the planet as an outpost of some importance for the interstellar community of all Earth-
descended men.

There were no flares of battle visible in space
around the planet, but still Liao lost no time in
transmitting a message on the standard radio and
laser communications frequencies. "Meitner's Planet,
calling Meitner's. This is the dreadnought *Hamilcar
Barca*. Are you under attack? Do you need immediate assistance?"

There came no immediate answer, nor could one
be expected for several minutes, the time required
for signals traveling at the speed of light to reach the
planet, and for an answer to be returned.

Into Liao's earphones now came the voice of his
Detection and Ranging Officer. "Captain, we have
three ships in view." On the bridge there now sprang
to life a three-dimensional holographic presentation,
showing Liao the situation as accurately as the dreadnought's far-ranging detection systems and elaborate
combat computers could diagram it. He smoothed
graying hair back from his high forehead with an

habitual gesture, and tried to determine what was going on.

One ship, appearing as a small bright dot with attached numerical coordinates, was hanging relatively motionless in space, nearly on a line between *Hamilcar Barca* and Meitner's Planet. The symbol chosen for it indicated that this was probably a sizable craft, though not nearly as massive as the dreadnought. The other two ships visible in the presentation were much smaller, according to the mass-detector readings on them. They were also both considerably closer to the planet, and moving toward it at velocities that would let them land on it, if that was their intention, in less than an hour.

What these three ships were up to, and whether they were controlled by human beings or berserker machines, was not immediately apparent. After sizing up the situation for a few seconds, Liao ordered full speed toward the planet—full speed, of course, in the sense of remaining in normal space and thus traveling much slower than light—and to each of the three ships in view he ordered the same message beamed: "Identify yourself, or be destroyed."

The threat was no bluff. No one took chances where berserker machines were concerned. They were an armada of robot spaceships and supporting devices built by some unknown and long-vanished race to fight in some interstellar war that had reached its forgotten conclusion while men on Earth were wielding spears against the sabertooth tiger. Though the war for which the berserker machines had been made was long since over, still they fought on across the galaxy, replicating and repairing themselves endlessly, learning new strategies and tactics, refining their weapons to cope with their chief new enemy,

Earth-descended man. The sole known basic in their fundamental programming was the destruction of all life, wherever and whenever they could find it.

Waiting for replies from the planet and the three ships, hoping fervently that the berserker fleet that was known to be on its way here had not already come and gone and left the helpless colony destroyed, Liao meanwhile studied his instruments critically. "Drive, this is the Captain. Can't you get a little more speed on?"

The answer came into his earphones: "No, sir, we're on the red line now. Another kilometer-per-second and we'll blow a power lamp or worse. This is one heavy sun, and it's got some dirty space around it." The ship was running now on the same space-warping engines that carried it faster than light between the stars, but this deep within the huge gravitational well surrounding Meitner's Sun the power that could be applied to them was severely restricted. The more so because here space was dirty, as the Drive Officer had said, meaning the interplanetary matter to be encountered within this system was comparatively dense. It boiled down to the fact that Liao had no hope of overtaking the two small vessels that fled ahead of him toward the planet. They, as it were, skimmed over shoals of particles that the dreadnought must plow through, flirted with reefs of drive-wrecking gravitational potential that it must approach more cautiously, and rode more lightly the waves of the solar wind that streamed outward as always from a sun.

Now the minimum time in which the largest, nearest vessel might have replied to the dreadnought's challenge had come and gone. No reply had been

received. Liao ordered the challenge repeated con-
tinuously.

The Communications Officer was speaking. "Answer from the planet, Captain. It's coming in code. I
mean the simple standard dot-dash code, sir, like the
emergency signals. There's a lot of noise around too,
maybe that's the only way they can get a signal
through." Powerfully and crudely modulated dot-and-
dash signals could carry intelligence through under
conditions where more advanced forms of modula-
tion were simply lost.

Communications was on the ball; already they had
the decoded words flowing across a big screen on the
bridge.

DREADNOUGHT ARE WE EVER GLAD TO HEAR FROM YOU
STOP ONE OF THE TWO LITTLE SHIPS CLOSING IN ON US
MUST BE A BERSERKER STOP BETTER TRANSMIT TO US IN
DOT-DASH CODE STOP LOTS OF NOISE BECAUSE SUN IS
FLARING AND WE COULDNT READ YOUR SIGNAL VERY
WELL

The letters abruptly stopped flowing across the
screen. The voice of the Communications Officer
said: "Big burst of noise, Captain, signals from the
planet are going to be cut off entirely for a little
while. This sun is a very active flare star . . . just a
moment, sir. Now we're getting voice and video
transmissions beamed to us from both small ships.
But the signals from both ships are so garbled by
noise we can't make anything out of them."

"Beam back to them in dot-dash, tell them they'll
have to answer us that way. Repeat our warnings
that they must identify themselves. And keep trying
to find out what the ground wants to tell us." The

Captain turned his head to look over at his Second Officer in the adjoining combat chair. "What'd you think of that, Miller? 'One of the two little ships must be a berserker'?"

Miller, by nature a somewhat morose man, only shook his massive head gloomily, knitted heavy brows, and saved his speech to make a factual report. "Sir, I've been working on identifying the two active ships. The one nearest the planet is so small it seems to be nothing more than a lifeboat. Extrapolating backward from its present course and position indicates it may well have come from the third ship, the one that's drifting, a couple of hours ago.

"The second little ship is a true interstellar vessel; could be a one-man courier ship or even somebody's private yacht. Or a berserker, of course." The enemy came in all shapes and sizes.

Still no answer had been returned from the large, drifting ship, though the dreadnought was continuing to beam threatening messages to her, now in dot-dash code. Detection reported now that she was spinning slowly around her longest axis, consistent with the theory that she was some kind of derelict. Liao checked again on the state of communications with the planet, but they were still cut off by noise.

"But here's something, Captain. Dot-and-dash is coming in from the supposed courier. Standard code as before, coming at moderate manual speed."

Immediately, more letters began to flow across the number-one screen on the bridge:

I AM METION CHONGJIN COMMANDING THE ONE MAN COURIER ETRURIA EIGHT DAYS OUT OF ESTEEL STOP CANNOT TURN ASIDE I AM CARRYING VITAL DEFENSE COMPONENT FOR COLONY STOP LIFEBOAT APPROX 12 MILLION

KM TO MY PORT AND AHEAD IS SAID BY GROUND TO BE
CLAIMING TO BE THE SHIP CARRYING THE DEFENSE COM-
PONENT THEREFORE IT MUST REALLY BE A BERSERKER
STOP IT WILL PROBABLY REACH COLONY AND BOMB OR
RAM IT BEFORE I GET THERE SO YOU MUST DESTROY
IT REPEAT DESTROY THE BERSERKER QUOTE LIFEBOAT
UNQUOTE MOST URGENT THAT YOU HIT IT SOON END
MESSAGE

Miller made a faint whistling noise. "Sounds fairly
convincing, Chief." During briefing back at base three
standard days ago they had been informed of the fact
that the colony on Meitner's Planet was awaiting
shipment of a space inverter to complete and activate
their defensive system of protective force-screens and
beam-projecting weapons. Until the inverter could
be brought from Esteel and installed the colony was
virtually defenseless; the dreadnought had been dis-
patched to offer it some interim protection.

Liao was giving orders to Armament to lock the
c-plus cannon of the main battery onto the lifeboat.
"But fire only on my command." Turning back to the
Second, he said: "Yes, fairly convincing. But the
berserkers might have found out somehow that the
space inverter was being rushed here. They might
even have intercepted and taken over the courier
carrying it. We can't see who we're talking to on that
ship or hear his voice. It might have been a berserker
machine that just tapped out that message to us."

The Communications Officer was on again. "Bridge,
we have the first coded reply from the lifeboat coming in now. Here it comes on your screen."

WE ARE HENRI SAKAI AND WINIFRED ISPAHAN CARRYING
THE DEFENSE MATERIEL NAMELY SPACE INVERTER THEY

NEED ON THE PLANET STOP OUR SHIP THE WILHELMINA
FROM ESTEEL WAS SHOT UP BY THE BERSERKER TWO
DAYS AGO WHEN IT ALMOST CAUGHT US STOP THE BER-
SERKER OR ANOTHER ONE IS HERE NOW ABOUT 11 MIL-
LION KM TO OUR STARBOARD AND A LITTLE BEHIND US
YOU MUST YOU MUST KEEP IT FROM GETTING TO US OR TO
THE PLANET WHERE MAYBE IT COULD RAM THE DOME
END MESSAGE

"Communications," the Captain snapped, "how is
this coming through? I mean, does this also seem
like someone sending manual code?"

"No, sir, this is very rapid and regular. But if you
mean, Captain, does that prove they're not human,
it doesn't. In a lifeboat the transmitter often has a
voice-to-code converter built in."

"And conversely a berserker could send slowly and
somewhat irregularly, like a man, if it wanted to.
Thank you." The Captain pondered in silence for a
little while.

"Sir," Miller suggested, "maybe we'd better order
both small ships to stop, until we can overtake and
board them."

The Captain turned his head to look at him steadily, but remained silent.

Miller, slightly flustered, took thought and then
corrected himself. "Now I see the problem more
fully, sir. You can't do that. If one of them is really
carrying the space inverter you don't dare delay him
for a minute. A berserker fleet may materialize in-
system here at any moment, and is virtually certain
to arrive within the next six to eight hours. Our ship
alone won't be able to do more than hit-and-run
when that happens. Our fleet can't get here for an-

other day. The colony will never survive the interval without their space inverter installed."

"Right. Even if I sent a fast launch ahead to board and inspect those ships, the delay would be too much to risk. And that's not all, Second. Tell me this—is this conceivably just some misunderstanding, and both of those ships are really manned by human beings?"

"Not a chance," the Second answered promptly. "They both claim to be carrying the space inverter, and that can't be true. Those things just aren't ordered or built in duplicate or triplicate, and they both claim to be bringing it from the planet Esteel . . . the next question is, can both of our little targets be berserkers? Trying to psych us into letting one of them get through? I'll keep trying to reach the ground, see if they can shed any more light on this." Miller swiveled away in his heavy chair.

"Good going."

In their earphones Communications said: "Here's more from the ship that calls itself *Etruria*, Bridge."

"Put it right on our screen."

REPEAT COLONY SAYS LIFEBOAT IS ALSO CLAIMING TO BE THE HUMAN ONE STOP THEY MUST BE A BERSERKER IMPERATIVE YOU STOP THEM WHAT DO YOU WANT ME TO DO TO PROVE IM HUMAN STOP REPEAT MY NAME IS METION CHONGJIN IM ALONE ON BOARD HERE WIFE AND KIDS AT HOME ON ESTEEL IF THAT MEANS ANYTHING TO YOU STOP REPEAT HOW CAN I PROVE TO YOU IM HUMAN END MESSAGE

"Easy," Captain Liao muttered to himself. "Father a human child. Compose a decent symphony. In the next forty minutes or so." That was approximately the

time left before at least one of the ships would be
able to reach the planet. Liao's mind was racing to
formulate possible tests, but getting nowhere. Berserkers had awesome powers, not only as physical
fighting machines, but as computers. They could not
counterfeit either human appearance or human behavior successfully when under close observation;
but Liao was not certain that a battery of psychologists with several days to work in would be able to
say with certainty whether it was a living man or a
lying berserker that answered their questions in
dot-dash.

Time passed. Hurtling through silence and near-
emptiness at many kilometers per second, the ships
very slowly changed the positions of their symbols in
the huge holographic presentation on the bridge.

"Now more from the *Wilhelmina*'s lifeboat, Captain."

"Run that on the top of the screen, will you, and
put any more that comes in from *Etruria* on the
bottom."

HENRI AND WINIFRED HERE COLONY TELLS US OTHER
SHIP IS CLAIMING TO BE FROM ESTEEL CARRYING DE-
FENSE COMPONENTS AND REQUESTING LANDING IN-
STRUCTIONS STOP IT MUST BE LYING IT MUST BE A BER-
SERKER MAYBE THE SAME ONE THAT ATTACKED OUR SHIP
TWO DAYS AGO . . .

The message ran on and despite some irrelevan-
cies and redundancies it outlined a coherent story.
The *Wilhelmina* (if the story was to be believed) had
been on an interstellar cruise, carrying a number of
young people on some kind of student exchange
voyage or post-graduate trip. Somewhere on the out-
skirts of the solar system that contained the heavily

industrialized planet Esteel, a courier ship bound for Meitner's had approached and hailed the *Wilhelmina*, had in fact commandeered her to complete the courier's mission. Berserkers were in pursuit of the courier and had already damaged her extensively.

... AND WE WERE ON OUR WAY HERE WITH THE IN-VERTER WHEN ONE OF THE BERSERKERS ALMOST CAUGHT UP AGAIN TWO STANDARD DAYS AGO STOP WILHELMINA WAS BADLY SHOT UP THEN CREW ALL KILLED WE ARE ONLY TWO LEFT ALIVE TWO HISTORY STUDENTS WE HAD TERRIBLE PROBLEMS ASTROGATING HERE BUT MADE IT STOP LIVING IN LIFEBOAT AND WORKING RIDDLED SHIP IN SPACESUITS YOU CANT STOP US NOW AFTER ALL WE HAVE BEEN THROUGH STOP YOU MUST DESTROY THE BER-SERKER SHIP WE WILL REACH PLANET BEFORE IT DOES I THINK BUT IT WILL BE ABLE TO HIT THE DOME BEFORE THE SPACE INVERTER CAN BE INSTALLED STOP WE ARE GOING TO KEEP SENDING UNTIL YOU ARE CONVINCED WE ARE HUMAN ...

The message from the lifeboat went on, somewhat more repetitiously now. And at the same time on the bottom of the screen more words from *Etruria* flowed in:

I HAVE TRIED TO CATCH THE BERSERKER LIFEBOAT AND SHOOT IT DOWN BUT I CANT ITS UP TO YOU TO STOP IT STOP WHAT DO YOU WANT ME TO DO TO PROVE IM HU-MAN ...

The Second Officer sighed lightly to himself, wondering if, after all, he really wanted his own command.

"Communications, beam this out," the Captain was ordering. "Tell them both to keep talking and give us their life histories. Birth, family, education, the works. Tell them both they'd better make it good if they want to live." On buttons on the arm of his chair he punched out an order for tea, and a moment later tea came to him there through a little door, hot in a capped cup with drinking tube attached. "I've got an idea. Second. You study the background this so-called Esteeler spaceman Metion Chongjin gives us. Think up someplace you might have known him. We'll introduce you to him as an old friend, see how he copes."

"Good idea, Chief."

"Communications here again, Bridge. We've finally gotten another clear answer back from the ground. It's coming through now, we'll put it in the middle of your number-one screen."

. . . IN ANSWER TO YOUR QUESTION NO THEY CANT BOTH BE BERSERKERS STOP AN HOUR AGO THERE WAS A BRIEF LETUP IN THE NOISE AND WE GOT ONE CLEAR LOOK AT A HUMAN MALE FACE ALIVE AND TALKING COGENTLY AN-SWERING OUR QUESTIONS NO POSSIBILITY THAT WAS A BERSERKER BUT UNFORTUNATELY BOTH SUSPECT SHIPS WERE SENDING ON THE SAME FREQ AND WE DONT KNOW FROM WHICH ONE THAT VOICE AND PICTURE CAME BUT WE DO KNOW THAT ONE OF THEM IS HUMAN . . .

"Damnation, how they've botched things up. Why didn't they ask the two men to describe themselves, and see which description fit what they saw?"

"This is Communications again, Bridge. They may have tried asking that, sir, for all we know. We've lost contact with the ground again now, even on code. I guess the solar wind is heating up. Conditions in the ionosphere down there must be pretty fierce. Anyway, here's a little more from the *Etruria*":

WHAT DO YOU WANT ME TO DO TO PROVE IM HUMAN RECITE POETRY MARY HAD A LITTLE LAMB STOP SAY PRAYERS I NEVER MEMORIZED ANY OF THEM STOP OKAY I GIVE UP SHOOT US BOTH DOWN THEN END MESSAGE

The Second Officer thumped a fist on the arm of his massive chair. "A berserker would say that, knowing that its fleet was coming, and the colony would be defenseless if we stopped the space inverter from getting to it."

Liao shrugged, and helped himself to a massive slug of tea. "But a human might say that too, being willing to die to give the colony a few more hours of life. A human might hope that given a few more hours some miracle might come along, like the human fleet getting here first after all. I'm afraid that statement didn't prove a thing."

"I . . . guess it didn't."

After another good slug of tea, Liao put in a call to Astrogation.

"Chief Astrogator here, sir."

"Barbara, have you been listening in on this? Good. Tell me, could those two supposed history students, probably knowing little science or technology, have brought that ship in here? Specifically, could they have astrogated for two days, maybe fifty or sixty light years, without getting lost? I suppose the ship's autopilot was knocked out. They said they were living in the lifeboat and working the damaged ship in spacesuits."

"Captain, I've been pondering that claim too, and I just don't know. I can't say definitely that it would be impossible. If we knew just how badly that ship was damaged, what they had to work with, we could make a better guess."

The Captain looked back at his situation hologram. The apparently inert hulk that he had been told was the *Wilhelmina* was considerably closer now, lying as it did almost in *Hamilcar Barca*'s path toward Meitner's Planet. The dreadnought was going to pass fairly near the other ship within the next few minutes. "As to that, maybe we can find out something. Keep listening in, Barbara." Turning to the Second Officer, Liao ordered: "You're going to be taking over the Bridge shortly, Miller. I want us to match velocities with that supposed hulk ahead, and then I'm going over to her, in hopes of learning something."

"It might be booby-trapped, Captain."

"Then we'll have an answer, won't we? But I don't expect an answer will be found that easily. Also get me a reading on exactly how much time we have left to decide which ship we're going to fire on."

"I've already had the computers going on that, sir. As of now, thirty-two and a quarter minutes. Then the lifeboat will either be down in atmosphere or around on the other side of the planet, and out of effective range in either case. The courier will take a little longer to get out of effective range, but . . ." He gestured helplessly.

"The courier being slower won't help us. We have to decide in thirty-two minutes."

"Chief, I just had an idea. If the lifeboat was the berserker, since it's closer to the planet, wouldn't it have tried before we got here to head off the courier from the planet . . . oh. No good. No offensive weapons on the lifeboat."

"Right, except perhaps it has one bloody big bomb,

meant for the colony. While the courier ship doubt-less has some light armament, enough to deal with the lifeboat if it got in range. Still nothing proven, either way."

In another minute the silent ship ahead was close enough for telescopes on the dreadnought to pick out her name by starlight. It was *Wilhelmina*, all right, emblazoned near one end of her cigarlike shape. The dreadnought matched velocities with her smoothly, and held position a couple of kilometers off. Just before getting into a launch with a squad of armed marines to go over and inspect her, Liao checked back with the Bridge to see if anything was new.

"Better hear this before you go," Miller told him. "I just introduced myself to Chongjin as an old buddy. This is his reply, quote: 'I honestly don't remember your name if I ever knew it, stop. If this was a test I guess I passed. Hurrah! Now get on with it and stop that berserker on the lifeboat . . .' and then the signal faded out again. Chief, our communication problems are getting steadily worse. If we're going to say anything more to either of those ships we'd better send it soon."

"How many minutes left, Second?"

"Just eighteen, sir."

"Don't waste any of 'em. This ship is yours."

"I relieve you, sir."

No signs of either life or berserker activity were apparent on the *Wilhelmina* as the launch crossed the space separating her from the dreadnought and docked, with a gentle clang of magnetic grapples. Now Liao could see that the reported damage was certainly a fact. Holes several meters in diameter had been torn in *Wilhelmina*'s outer hull. Conditions inside could hardly be good.

Leaving one man with the launch, Liao led the rest of his small party in through one of the blasted holes, swimming weightlessly, propelling themselves by whatever they could grip. He had briefed the men to look for something, anything, that would prove or disprove the contention that humans had driven this ship for the last two days since she had been damaged.

Fifteen and a half minutes left.

The damage inside was quite as extensive as the condition of the hull had indicated. Their suit lights augmenting the sharp beams that Meitner's distant sun threw into the airless interior, the boarding party spread out, keeping in touch by means of their suit radios. This had undoubtedly been a passenger ship. Much of the interior was meant as living quarters, divided into single and double cabins, with accommodations for a couple of dozen people. What furnishings remained suggested luxury. So far, everything said by the lifeboat's occupant was being proved true, but Liao as yet had no clear evidence regarding that occupant's humanity, nor even a firm idea of what evidence he was looking for. He only hoped that it was here, and that he would recognize it at first sight.

The interior of the ship was totally airless now, having been effectively opened to the stars by the repeated use of some kind of penetration weapon. The ruin was much cleaner than any similarly damaged structure on a planet's surface could be, loose debris having been carried out of the ship with escaping air, or separated from her when her drive took her outside of normal space and time, between the stars.

"Look here, Captain." The Lieutenant in charge of

the marine squad was beckoning to him. Liao followed, on a vertiginous twisting passage through the wreck.

Near the center of the slender ship the Lieutenant had found a place where a wound bigger than any of the others had pierced in, creating in effect an enormous skylight over what had been one of the largest compartments on board. Probably it had been a lounge or refectory for the passengers and crew. Since the ship was damaged this ruined room had evidently provided the most convenient observation platform for whoever or whatever had been in control: a small, wide-angle telescope, and a tubular electronic spectroscope, battery-powered and made for use in vacuum, had been roughly but effectively clamped to the jagged upper edge of what had been one of the lounge's interior walls and now formed a parapet against infinity.

The Lieutenant was swiveling the instruments on their mountings. "Captain, these look like emergency equipment from a lifeboat. Would a berserker machine have needed to use these, or would it have gear of its own?"

The Captain stood beside him. "When a berserker puts a prize crew on a ship, it uses man-sized, almost android machines for the job. It's just more convenient for the machines that way, more efficient. So they could quite easily use instruments designed for humans." He swung his legs to put his magnetic boots against the lounge's soft floor, so that they held him lightly to the steel deck beneath, and stared at the instruments, trying to force more meaning from them.

Men kept on searching the ship, probing everywhere, coming and going to report results (or rather the lack of them) to Liao at his impromptu command post in what had been the lounge. Two marines had broken open a jammed door and found a small airless room containing a dead man who wore a spacesuit; cause of death was not immediately apparent, but the uniform collar visible through the helmet's faceplate indicated that the man had been a member of *Wilhelmina*'s crew. And in an area of considerable damage near the lounge another, suitless, body was discovered wedged among twisted structural members. This corpse had probably been frozen near absolute zero for several days and exposed to vacuum for an equal length of time. Also its death had been violent. After all this it was hard to be sure, but Liao thought that the body had once been that of a young girl who had been wearing a fancy party dress when she met her end.

Liao could imagine a full scenario now, or rather two of them. Both began with the shipload of students, eighteen or twenty of them perhaps, enjoying their interstellar trip. Surely such a cruise had been a momentous event in their lives. Maybe they had been partying as they either entered or were about to leave the solar system containing the planet Esteel. And then, according to Scenario One, out of the deep night of space came the desperate plea for help from the damaged and harried courier, hotly pursued by berserkers that were not thought to be in this part of the galaxy at all.

The students would have had to remain on board the *Wilhelmina*, there being no place for them to get off, when she was commandeered to carry the space inverter on to Meitner's Planet. Then urgent flight, and two days from Meitner's a berserker almost catching up, tracking and finding and shooting holes in

Wilhelmina, somewhere in the great labyrinth of space and dust and stars and time, in which the little worlds of men were strange and isolated phenomena. And then the two heroic survivors, Henri and Winifred, finding a way to push on somehow.

Scenario Two diverged from that version early on, and was simpler and at first glance more credible. Instead of the *Wilhelmina* being hailed by a courier and pressed into military service, she was simply jumped by berserkers somewhere, her crew and passengers efficiently wiped out, her battered body driven on here ahead of the main berserker fleet in a ploy to forestall the installation of the space inverter and demolish the colony before any help could reach it. Scenario One was more heroic and romantic, Two more prosaic and businesslike. The trouble was that the real world was not committed to behaving in either style but went on its way indifferently.

A man was just now back from inspecting *Wilhelmina*'s control room. "Almost a total loss in there, sir, except for the Drive controls and their directional settings. Artificial gravity's gone, Astrogator's position is wiped out, and the autopilot too. Drive itself seems all right, as far as I can tell without trying it."

"Don't bother. Thank you, mister."

Another man came to report, drifting upside-down before the captain in the lack of gravity. "Starboard forward lifeboat's been launched, Captain. Others are all still in place, no signs of having been lived in. Eight-passenger models."

"Thank you," Liao said courteously. These facts told him nothing new. Twelve minutes left now, before he must select a target and give the command to fire. In his magnetic boots he stood before the telescope and spectroscope as their user had done, and looked out at the stars.

The slow rotation of the *Wilhelmina* brought the dreadnought into view, and Liao flicked his suit radio to the intership channel. "Bridge, this is Captain. Someone tell me just how big that space inverter is. Could two untrained people manhandle it and its packing into one of those little eight-passenger lifeboats?"

"This is the Armaments Officer, sir," an answer came back promptly. "I used to work in ground installations, and I've handled those things. I could put my arms around the biggest space inverter ever made, and it wouldn't mass more than fifty kilograms. It's not the size makes 'em rare and hard to come by, it's the complexity. Makes a regular drive unit or artificial gravity generator look like nothing."

"All right. Thank you. Astrogation, are you there?"

"Listening in, sir."

"Good. Barbara, the regular astrogator's gear on this ship seems to have been wiped out. What we have then is two history students or whatever, with unknown astronomical competence, working their way here from someplace two days off, in a series of *c*-plus jumps. We've found their instruments, apparently all they used, simple telescope and spectroscope. You've been thinking it over, now how about it? Possible?"

There was a pause. Barbara would be tapping at her console with a pencil. "Possible, yes. I can't say more than that on what you've given me."

"I'm not convinced it's possible. With umpteen thousand stars to look at, their patterns changing every time you jump, how could you hope to find the one you wanted to work toward?" *Ten minutes.* Inspiration struck. "Listen! Why couldn't they have shoved off in the lifeboat, two days ago, and used its autopilot?"

Barbara's voice was careful as always. "To answer your last question first, Chief, lifeboats on civilian ships are usually not adjustable to give you a choice of goals; they just bring you out in the nearest place where you are likely to be found. No good for either people or berserkers intent on coming to Meitner's system. And if *Wilhelmina*'s drive is working it could take them between the stars faster than a lifeboat could.

"To answer your first question, the lifeboats carry aids for the amateur astrogator, such as spectral records of thousands of key stars, kept on microfilm. Also often provided is an electronic scanning spectroscope of the type you seem to have found there. The star records are indexed by basic spectral type, you know, types O, B, A, F, G, K, and so on. Type O stars, for example, are quite rare in this neck of the woods so if you just scanned for them you would cut down tremendously on the number of stars to be looked at closely for identification. There are large drawbacks to such a system of astrogation, but on the other hand with a little luck one might go a long way using it. If the two students are real people, though, I'll bet at least one of them knows some astronomy."

"Thank you," Liao said carefully, once again. He glanced around him. The marines were still busy, flashing their lights on everything and poking into every crevice. *Eight minutes.* He thought he could keep the time in his head now, not needing any artificial chronometer.

People had lived in this lounge, or rec room, or

whatever it had been, and enjoyed themselves. The wall to which the astrogation instruments were now fastened had earlier been decorated, or burdened, with numerous graffiti of the kinds students seemed always to generate. Many of the messages, Liao saw now, were in English, an ancient and honorable language still fairly widely taught. From his own schooldays he remembered enough to be able to read it fairly well, helping himself out with an occasional guess.

CAPTAIN AHAB CHASES ALEWIVES, said one message proceeding boldly across the wall at an easy reading height. The first and third words of that were certainly English, but the meaning of the whole eluded him. Captain Liao chases shadows, he thought, and hunches. What else is left?

Here was another:

OSS AND HIS NOBLE CLASSMATES WISH THE WHOLE WORLD

And then nothingness, the remainder of the message having gone when Oss and his noble classmates went and the upper half of this wall went with them.

"Here, Captain! Look!" A marine was beckoning wildly.

The writing he was pointing to was low down on the wall and inconspicuous, made with a thinner writing instrument than most of the other graffiti had been. It said simply: *Henri & Winifred*.

Liao looked at it, first with a jumping hope in his heart and then with a sagging sensation that had rapidly become all too familiar. He rubbed at the writing with his suited thumb; nothing much came off. He said: "Can anyone tell me in seven minutes whether this was put here after the air went out of the ship? If so, it would seem to prove that Henri and Winifred were still around then. Otherwise it proves nothing." If the berserker had been here it could easily have seen those names and retained them in its effortless, lifeless memory, and used them when it had to construct a scenario.

"Where are Henri and Winifred now, that is the question," Liao said to the Lieutenant, who came drifting near, evidently wondering, as they all must be, what to do next. "Maybe that was Winifred back there in the party dress."

The marine answered: "Sir, that might have been Henri, for all that I could tell." He went on directing his men, and waiting for the Captain to tell him what else was to be done.

A little distance to one side of the names, an English message in the same script and apparently made with the same writing instrument went down the wall like this:

Oh	*Kiss*
Be	*Me*
A	*Right*
Fine	*Now*
Girl	*Sweetie*

Liao was willing to bet that particular message wasn't written by anyone wearing a space helmet. But no, he wouldn't make such a bet, not really. If he tried he could easily enough picture the two young people rubbing faceplates and laughing, momentarily able to forget the dead wedged in the twisted girders a few meters away. Something about that message nagged at his memory, though. Could it be the first line of an English poem he had forgotten?

The slow turn of the torn ship was bringing the dreadnought into view again. "Bridge, this is Captain. Tell me anything that's new."

"Sir, here's a little more that came in clear from the lifeboat. I quote: 'This is Winifred talking now, stop. We're going on being human even if you don't believe us, stop.' Some more repetitious stuff, Captain, and then this: 'While Henri was navigating I would come out from the lifeboat with him and he started trying to teach me about the stars, stop. We wrote our names there on the wall under the telescope; if you care to look you'll find them; of course that doesn't prove anything, does it. If I had lenses for eyes I could have read those names there and remembered them . . .' It cuts off again there, Chief, buried in noise."

"Second, confirm my reading of how much time we have left to decide."

"Three minutes and forty seconds, sir. That's cutting it thin."

"Thanks." Liao fell silent, looking off across the universe. If offered him no help.

"Sir! Sir! I may have something here." It was the marine who had found the names, who was still closely examining the wall.

Looking at the wall where the man had aimed his helmet light, near the deck below the mounted instruments, Liao beheld a set of small grayish indented scratches, about half a meter apart.

"Sir, some machine coming here repeatedly to use the scopes might well have made these markings on the wall. Whereas a man or woman in spacesuits would not have left such marks, in my opinion, sir."

"I see." Looking at the marks, that might have been made by anything, maybe furniture banged into the wall during that final party, Liao felt an irrational anger at the marine. But of course the man was only trying to help. He had a duty to put forward any possibly useful idea that came into his head. "I'm not sure these were made by a berserker, spaceman, but it's something to think about. How much time have we left, Second?"

"Just under three minutes, sir. Standing by ready to fire at target of your choice, sir. Pleading messages still coming in intermittently from both ships, nothing new in them."

"All right." The only reasonable hope of winning was to guess and take the fifty-fifty chance. If he let both ships go on, the bad one was certain to ram into the colony and destroy it before the other could deliver the key to the defenses and it could be installed. If he destroyed both ships, the odds were ten to one or worse that the berserker fleet would be here shortly and accomplish the same ruin upon a colony deprived of any chance of protecting itself.

Liao adjusted his throat muscles so that his voice when it came out would be firm and certain, and then he flipped a coin in his mind. Well, not really. There were the indented scratches on the bulkhead, perhaps not so meaningless after all, and there was the story of the two students' struggle to get here, perhaps a little too fantastic. "Hit the lifeboat," he said then, decisively. "Give it another two minutes, but if no new evidence turns up, let go at it with the main turret. Under no circumstances delay enough to let it reach the planet."

"Understand, sir," said Miller's voice. "Fire at the lifeboat two minutes from your order."

He would repeat the order to fire, emphatically, when the time was up, so that there could be no possible confusion as to where responsibility lay. "Lieutenant, let's get the men back to the launch. Continue to keep your eyes open on the way, for anything . . ."

"Yes, sir."

The last one to leave the ruined lounge-observatory, Liao looked at the place once more before following the marines back through the ship. *Oh, be a fine girl, Winifred, when the slug from the c-plus cannon comes. But if I have guessed wrong and it is coming for you, at least you'll never see it. Just no more for you. No more Henri and no more lessons about the stars.*

The stars . . .

Oh, be a fine girl . . .

O, B, A, F, G, K, . . .

"*Second Officer!*"

"Sir!"

"Cancel my previous order! Let the lifeboat land. Hit the *Etruria*! Unload on that bloody damned berserker with everything we've got, right now!"

"Yessir!"

Long before Liao got back to the launch the *c*-plus cannon volleyed. Their firing was invisible, and inaudible here in airlessness, but still he and the others felt the energies released pass twistily through all their bones. Now the huge leaden slugs would begin skipping in and out of normal space, homing on their tiny target, far out-racing light in their trajectories toward Meitner's Planet. The slugs would be traveling now like de Broglie wavicles, one aspect matter with its mass magnified awesomely by Einsteinian velocity, one aspect waves of not much more than mathematics. The molecules of lead churned internally with phase velocities greater than that of light.

Liao was back on the dreadnought's bridge before laggard light brought the faint flash of destruction back.

"Direct hit, Captain." There was no need to amplify on that.

"Good shots, Arms."

And then, only a little later, a message got through the planet's ionospheric noise to tell them that the two people with the space inverter were safely down.

Within a few hours the berserker fleet appeared in system, found an armed and ready colony, with *Hamilcar Barca* hanging by for heavy hit-and-run support, skirmished briefly and then decided to decline battle and departed. A few hours after that, the human fleet arrived and decided to pause for some refitting. And then Captain Liao had a chance to get down into the domed colony and talk to two people who wanted very much to meet him.

"So," he was explaining, soon after the first round of mutual congratulations had been completed, "when I at last recognized the mnemonic on the wall for what it was, I knew that not only had Henri and Winny been there but that he had in fact been teaching her something about astronomical spectroscopy at that very place beside the instruments— therefore after the ship was damaged."

Henri was shaking his youthful head, with the air of one still marveling at it all. "Yes, *now* I can remember putting the mnemonic thing down, showing her how to remember the order of spectral types. I guess we use mnemonics all the time without thinking about it much. *Every good boy does fine,* for the musical notes. *Bad boys race our young girls*—that one's in electronics."

The captain nodded. "*Thirty days hath September.* And *Barbara Celarent* that the logicians still use now and then. Berserkers, with their perfect memories, probably don't even know what mnemonics are, much less need them. Anyway, if the berserker had been on the *Wilhelmina,* it would've had no reason to leave false clues. No way it could have guessed that I was coming to look things over."

Winifred, slender and too fragile-looking for what she had been through, took him by the hand. "Captain, you've given us our lives, you know. What can we ever do for you?"

"Well. For a start . . ." He slipped into some English he had recently practiced: "You might be a fine girl, sweetie, and . . ."

And the search for truth may be the lifework of a human mind. Praise be to those who have such a purpose—truly—in their hearts!

SOME EVENTS AT THE TEMPLAR RADIANT

All his years of past work, and more than that, his entire future too, hung balanced on this moment.

A chair forgotten somewhere behind him, Sabel stood tall in the blue habit that often served him as laboratory coat. His hands gripped opposite corners of the high, pulpit-like control console. His head was thrown back, eyes closed, sweat-dampened dark hair hanging in something more than its usual disarray over his high, pale forehead.

He was alone, as far as any other human presence was concerned. The large, stone-walled chamber in which he stood was for the moment quiet.

All his years of work . . . and although during the past few days he had mentally rehearsed this moment to the point of exhaustion, he was still uncertain of how to start. Should he begin with a series of cautious, testing questions, or ought he leap toward his real goal at once?

Hesitancy could not be long endured, not now. But caution, as it usually had during his mental rehearsals, prevailed.

Eyes open, Sabel faced the workbenches filled with

87

equipment that were arranged before him. Quietly
he said: "You are what human beings call a berserker. Confirm or deny."

"Confirm." The voice was familiar, because his
hookup gave it the same human-sounding tones in
which his own laboratory computer ordinarily spoke
to him. It was a familiarity that he must not allow to
become in the least degree reassuring.

So far, at least, success. "You understand," Sabel
pronounced, "that I have restored you from a state of
nearly complete destruction. I—"

"Destruction," echoed the cheerful workbench
voice.

"Yes. You understand that you no longer have the
power to destroy, to take life. That you are now
constrained to answer all my—"

"To take life."

"Yes. Stop interrupting me." He raised a hand to
wipe a trickle of fresh sweat from an eye. He saw
how his hand was quivering with the strain of its
unconscious grip upon the console. "Now," he said,
and had to pause, trying to remember where he was
in his plan of questioning.

Into the pause, the voice from his laboratory speakers said: "In you there is life."

"There is." Sabel managed to reassert himself, to
pull himself together. "Human life." Dark eyes glaring steadily across the lab, he peered at the long,
cabled benches whereon his captive enemy lay
stretched, bound down, vitals exposed like those of
some hapless human on a torture rack. Not that he
could torture what had no nerves and did not live.
Nor was there anything like a human shape in sight.
All that he had here of the berserker was fragmented.
One box here, another there, between them a chem-

ical construct in a tank, that whole complex wired to
an adjoining bench that bore rows of semi-material
crystals.

Again his familiar laboratory speaker uttered alien
words: "Life is to be destroyed."

This did not surprise Sabel; it was only a restate-
ment of the basic programmed command that all
berserkers bore. They were machines fabricated by
unknown builders on an unknown world, at a time
perhaps before any creature living on Earth had
been able to see stars as anything more than points
of light. That the statement was made so boldly now
roused in Sabel nothing but hope; it seemed that at
least the thing was not going to begin by trying to lie
to him.

It seemed also that he had established a firm physical control. Scanning the indicators just before him
on the console, he saw no sign of danger . . . he
knew that, given the slightest chance, his prisoner
was going to try to implement its basic programming. He had of course separated it from anything
obviously useful as a weapon. But he was not absolutely certain of the functions of all the berserker
components that he had brought into his laboratory
and hooked up. And the lab of course was full of
potential weapons. There were fields, electric and
otherwise, quite powerful enough to extinguish human life. There were objects that could be turned
into deadly projectiles by only a very moderate ap-
plication of force. To ward off any such improvisa-
tions Sabel had set defensive rings of force to dancing
round the benches upon which his foe lay bound.
And, just for insurance, another curtain of fields
hung round him and the console. The fields were
almost invisible, but the ancient stonework of the

lab's far wall kept acquiring and losing new flavorings of light at the spots where the spinning field-components brushed it and eased free again.

Not that it seemed likely that the berserker-brain in its present disabled and almost disembodied state could establish control over weaponry enough to kill a mouse. Nor did Sabel ordinarily go overboard on the side of caution. But, as he told himself, he understood very well just what he was dealing with.

He had paused again, seeking reassurance from the indicators ranked before him. All appeared to be going well, and he went on: "I seek information from you. It is not military information, so whatever inhibitions have been programmed into you against answering human questions do not apply." Not that he felt at all confident that a berserker would meekly take direction from him. But there was nothing to be lost by the attempt.

The reply from the machine was delayed longer than he had expected, so that he began to hope his attempt had been successful. But then the answer came.

"I may trade certain classes of information to you, in return for lives to be destroyed."

The possibility of some such proposition had crossed Sabel's mind some time ago. In the next room a cage of small laboratory animals was waiting.

"I am a cosmophysicist," he said. "In particular I strive to understand the Radiant. In the records of past observations of the Radiant there is a long gap that I would like to fill. This gap corresponds to the period of several hundred standard years during which berserkers occupied this fortress. That period ended with the battle in which you were severely damaged. Therefore I believe that your memory probably contains some observations that will be very useful to me. It is not necessary that they be formal observations of the Radiant. Any scene recorded in light from the Radiant may be helpful. Do you understand?"

"In return for my giving you such records, what lives am I offered to destroy?"

"I can provide several." Eagerly Sabel once more swept his gaze along his row of indicators. His recording instruments were probing hungrily, gathering at an enormous rate the data needed for at least a partial understanding of the workings of his foe's unliving brain. At a score of points their probes were fastened in its vitals.

"Let me destroy one now," its human-sounding voice requested.

"Presently. I order you to answer one question for me first."

"I am not constrained to answer any of your questions. Let me destroy a life."

Sabel turned a narrow doorway for himself through his defensive fields, and walked through it into the next room. In a few seconds he was back. "Can you see what I am carrying?"

"Then it is not a human life you offer me."

"That would be utterly impossible."

"Then it is utterly impossible for me to give you information."

Without haste he turned and went to put the animal back into the cage. He had expected there might well be arguments, bargaining. But this argument was only the first level of Sabel's attack. His data-gathering instruments were what he really counted on. The enemy doubtless knew that it was being probed and analyzed. But there was evidently nothing it could do about it. As long as Sabel supplied it power, its brain must remain functional. And while it functioned, it must try to devise ways to kill.

Back at his console, Sabel took more readings. DATA PROBABLY SUFFICIENT FOR ANALYSIS, his computer screen at last informed him. He let out breath with a sigh of satisfaction, and at once threw certain switches, letting power die. Later if necessary he could turn the damned thing on again and argue with it some more. Now his defensive fields vanished, leaving him free to walk between the workbenches, where he stretched his aching back and shoulders in silent exultation.

Just as an additional precaution, he paused to disconnect a cable. The demonic enemy was only hardware now. Precisely arranged atoms, measured molecules, patterned larger bits of this and that. Where now was the berserker that humanity so justly feared? That had given the Templars their whole reason for existence? It no longer existed except in potential. Take the hardware apart, on even the finest level, and you would not discover any of its memories. But, reconnect this and that, reapply power here and there, and back it would bloom into reality, as malignant and clever and full of information as before. A non-material artifact of matter. A pattern.

No way existed, even in theory, to torture a machine into compliance, to extort information from it. Sabel's own computers were using the Van Holt algorithms, the latest pertinent mathematical advance. Even so they could not entirely decode the concealing patterns, the trapdoor functions, by which the berserker's memory was coded and concealed. The largest computer in the human universe would probably not have time for that before the universe itself came to an end. The unknown Builders had built well.

But there were other ways besides pure mathematics with which to circumvent a cipher. Perhaps, he thought, he would have tried to find a way to offer it a life, had that been the only method he could think of.

Certainly he was going to try another first. There had to be, he thought, some way of disabling the lethal purpose of a berserker while leaving its calculating abilities and memory intact. There would have been times when the living Builders wanted to approach their creations, at least in the lab, to test them and work on them. Not an easy or simple way, perhaps, but something. And that way Sabel now instructed his own computers to discover, using the mass of data just accumulated by measuring the berserker in operation.

Having done that, Sabel stood back and surveyed his laboratory carefully. There was no reason to think that anyone else was going to enter it in the near future, but it would be stupid to take chances. To the Guardians, an experiment with viable berserker parts would stand as *prima facie* evidence of goodlife activity; and in the Templar code, as in many another system of human law, any such willing service of the berserker cause was punishable by death.

Only a few of the materials in sight might be incriminating in themselves. Coldly thoughtful, Sabel made more disconnections, and rearrangements. Some things he locked out of sight in cabinets, and from the cabinets he took out other things to be incorporated in a new disposition on the benches. Yes, this was certainly good enough. He suspected that most of the Guardians probably no longer knew what the insides of a real berserker looked like.

Sabel made sure that the doors leading out of the lab, to the mall-level corridor, and to his adjoining living quarters, were both locked. Then, whistling faintly, he went up the old stone stair between the skylights, that brought him out upon the glassed-in roof.

Here he stood bathed in the direct light of the Radiant itself. It was a brilliant point some four kilometers directly above his head—the pressure of the Radiant's inverse gravity put it directly overhead for everyone in the englobing structure of the Fortress. It was a point brighter than a star but dimmer than a sun, not painful to look at. Around Sabel a small forest of sensors, connected to instruments in his laboratory below, raised panels and lenses in a blind communal stare, to that eternal noon. Among these he began to move about as habit led him, mechanically checking the sensors' operation, though for once he was not really thinking about the Radiant at all. He thought of his success below. Then once more he raised his own two human eyes to look.

It made its own sky, out of the space enclosed by the whitish inner surface of the Fortress's bulk. Sabel could give from memory vastly detailed expositions of the spectrum of the Radiant's light. But as to exactly what color it was, in terms of perception by the eye and brain—well, there were different judgments on that, and for his part he was still uncertain.

Scattered out at intervals across the great curve of interior sky made by the Fortress's whitish stonework, Sabel could see other glass portals like his own. Under some of them, other people would be looking up and out, perhaps at him. Across a blank space on the immense concavity, an echelon of maintenance machines were crawling, too far away for him to see what they were working at. And, relatively nearby, under the glass roof of a great ceremonial plaza, something definitely unusual was going on. A crowd of thousands of people, exceptional at any time in the Fortress with its relatively tiny population, were gathered in a circular mass, like live cells attracted to some gentle biological magnet at their formation's center.

Sabel had stared at this peculiarity for several seconds, and was reaching for a small telescope to probe it with, when he recalled that today was the Feast of Ex. Helen, which went a long way toward providing an explanation. He had in fact deliberately chosen this holiday for his crucial experiment, knowing that the Fortress's main computer would today be freed of much routine business, its full power available for him to tap if necessary.

And in the back of his mind he had realized also that he should probably put in an appearance at at least one of the day's religious ceremonies. But this gathering in the plaza—he could not recall that any ceremony, in the years since he had come to the Fortress, had ever drawn a comparable crowd.

Looking with his telescope up through his own glass roof and down through the circular one that sealed the plaza in from airless space, he saw that the crowd was centered on the bronze statue of Ex. Helen there. And on a man standing in a little cleared space before the statue, a man with arms raised as if to address the gathering. The angle was wrong for Sabel to get a good look at his face, but the blue and purple robes made the distant figure unmistakable.

It was the Potentate, come at last to the Fortress in his seemingly endless tour of his many subject worlds.

Sabel could not recall, even though he now made an effort to do so, that any such visitation had been impending—but then of late Sabel had been even more than usually isolated in his own work. The visit had practical implications for him, though, and he was going to have to find out more about it quickly. Because the agenda of any person of importance visiting the Fortress was very likely to include at some point a full-dress inspection of Sabel's own laboratory.

He went out through the corridor leading from laboratory to pedestrian mall, locking up carefully behind him, and thinking to himself that there was no need to panic. The Guardians would surely call to notify him that a visit by the Potentate impended, long before it came. It was part of their job to see that such things went smoothly, as well as to protect the Potentate while he was here. Sabel would have some kind of official warning. But this was certainly an awkward time . . .

Along the pedestrian mall that offered Sabel his most convenient route to the ceremonial plaza, some of the shops were closed—a greater number than usual for a holiday, he thought. Others appeared to be tended only by machines. In the green parkways that intersected the zig-zag mall at irregular intervals, there appeared to be fewer strollers than on an ordinary day. And the primary school operated by the Templars had evidently been closed; a minor explosion of youngsters in blue-striped coveralls darted across the mall from parkway to playground just ahead of Sabel, their yells making him wince.

When you stood at one side of the great plaza and looked across, both the convexity of its glass roof and the corresponding concavity of the level-feeling floor beneath were quite apparent. Especially now that the crowd was gone again. By the time Sabel reached the center of the plaza, the last of the Potentate's entourage were vanishing through exits on its far side.

Sabel was standing uncertainly on the lowest marble step of Ex. Helen's central shrine. Her statbronze statue dominated the plaza's center. Helen the Exemplar, Helen of the Radiant, Helen Dardan. The statue was impressive, showing a woman of extreme beauty in a toga-like Dardanian garment, a diadem on her short curly hair. Of course long-term dwellers at the Fortress ignored it for the most part, because of its sheer familiarity. Right now, though, someone was stopping to look, gazing up at the figure with intent appreciation.

Sabel's attention, in turn, gradually became concentrated upon this viewer. She was a young, brown-haired girl of unusually good figure, and clad in a rather provocative civilian dress.

And presently he found himself approaching her. "Young woman? If you would excuse my curiosity?"

The girl turned to him. With a quick, cheerful curiosity of her own she took in his blue habit, his stature, and his face. "No excuse is needed, sir." Her voice was musical. "What question can I answer for you?"

Sabel paused a moment in appreciation. Everything about this girl struck him as quietly delightful. Her manner held just a hint of timidity, compounded with a seeming eagerness to please.

Then he gestured toward the far side of the plaza.

"I see that our honored Potentate is here with us today. Do you by any chance know how long he plans to stay at the Fortress?"

The girl replied: "I heard someone say, ten standard days. It was one of the women wearing purple-bordered cloaks—?" She shook brown ringlets, and frowned with pretty regret at her own ignorance.

"Ah—one of the vestals. Perhaps you are a visitor here yourself?"

"A newcomer, rather. Isn't it always the way, sir, when you ask someone for local information? 'I'm a newcomer here myself.'"

Sabel chuckled. *Forget the Potentate for now.* "Well, I can hardly plead newcomer status. It must be something else that keeps me from knowing what goes on in my own city. Allow me to introduce myself: Georgicus Sabel, Doctor of Cosmography."

"Greta Thamar." Her face was so pretty, soft, and young, a perfect match for her scantily costumed body. She continued to radiate an almost-timid eagerness. "Sir, Dr. Sabel, would you mind if I asked you a question about yourself?"

"Ask anything."

"Your blue robe. That means you are one of the monks here?"

"I belong to the Order of Ex. Helen. The word 'monk' is not quite accurate."

"And the Order of Ex. Helen is a branch of the Templars, isn't it?"

"Yes. Though our Order is devoted more to contemplation and study than to combat."

"And the Templars in turn are a branch of Christianity."

"Or they were." Sabel favored the girl with an approving smile. "You are more knowledgeable than many newcomers. And, time was when many Templars really devoted themselves to fighting, as did their ancient namesakes."

The girl's interest continued. By some kind of body-language agreement the two of them had turned around and were now strolling slowly back in the direction that Sabel had come from.

Greta said: "I don't know about that. The ancient ones, I mean. Though I tried to study up before I came here. Please, go on."

"Might I ask your occupation, Greta?"

"I'm a dancer. Only on the popular entertainment level, I'm afraid. Over at the *Contrat Rouge*. But I . . . please, go on."

On the Templar-governed Fortress, popular entertainers were far down on the social scale. *Seen talking to a dancer in the plaza* . . . but no, there was really nothing to be feared from that. A minimal loss of status, perhaps, but counterbalanced by an increase in his more liberal acquaintances' perception of him as more fully human. All this slid more or less automatically through Sabel's mind, while the attractive smile on his face did not, or so he trusted, vary in the slightest.

Strolling on, he shrugged. "Perhaps there's not a great deal more to say, about the Order. We study and teach. Oh, we still officially garrison this Fortress. Those of us who are Guardians maintain and man the weapons, and make berserkers their field of study, besides acting as the local police. The main defenses out on the outer surface of the Fortress are still operational, though a good many decades have passed since we had a genuine alarm. There are no longer many berserkers in this part of the Galaxy." He smiled wryly. "And I am afraid there are no longer very many Templars, either, even in the parts of the Galaxy where things are not so peaceful."

They were still walking. Proceeding in the direction of Sabel's laboratory and quarters.

"Please, tell me more." The girl continued to look at him steadily with attention. "Please, I am really very interested."

"Well. We of the Order of Ex. Helen no longer bind ourselves to poverty—or to permanent celibacy. We have come to honor Beauty on the same level as Virtue, considering them both to be aspects of the Right. Our great patroness of course stands as Exemplar of both qualities."

"Ex. Helen . . . and she really founded the Order, hundreds of years ago? Or—"

"Or, is she really only a legend, as some folk now consider her? No. I think that there is really substantial evidence of her historical reality. Though of course the purposes of the Order are still valid in either case."

"You must be very busy. I hope you will forgive my taking up your time like this."

"It is hard to imagine anyone easier to forgive. Now, would you by chance like to see something of my laboratory?"

"Might I? Really?"

"You have already seen the Radiant, of course. But to get a look at it through some of my instruments will give you a new perspective . . ."

As Sabel had expected, Greta did not seem able to understand much of his laboratory's contents. But she was nevertheless impressed. "And I see you have a private space flyer here. Do you use it to go out to the Radiant?"

At that he really had to laugh. "I'm afraid I wouldn't get there. Oh, within a kilometer of it, maybe, if I tried. The most powerful spacecraft built might be able to force its way to within half that distance. But to approach any closer than that—impossible. You see, the inner level of the Fortress, where we are now, was built at the four-kilometer distance from the Radiant because that is the distance at which the effective gravity is standard normal. As one tries to get closer, the gravitic resistance goes up exponentially. No, I use the flyer for field trips. To the outer reaches of the Fortress, places where no public transport is available."

"Is that a hobby of some kind?"

"No, it's really connected with my work. I search for old Dardanian records, trying to find their observations of the Radiant . . . and in here is where I live."

With eyes suddenly become competent, Greta surveyed the tidy smallness of his quarters. "Alone, I see."

"Most of the time . . . my work demands so much. Now, Greta, I have given you something of a private showing of my work. I would be very pleased indeed if you were willing to do the same for me."

"To dance?" Her manner altered, in a complex way. "I suppose there might be room enough in here for dancing . . . if there were some suitable music."

"Easily provided." He found a control on the wall; and to his annoyance he noticed that his fingers were now quivering again.

In light tones Greta said: "I have no special costume with me, sir, just these clothes I wear."

"They are delightful—but you have one other, surely."

"Sir?" And she, with quick intelligence in certain fields of thought, was trying to repress a smile.

"Why, my dear, I mean the costume that nature gives to us all, before our clothes are made. Now, if it is really going to be up to me to choose . . ."

Hours later when the girl was gone, he went back to work, this time wearing a more conventional laboratory coat. He punched in a command for his computer to display its results, and, holding his breath, looked at the screen.

BASIC PROGRAMMING OF SUBJECT DEVICE MAY BE CIRCUMVENTED AS FOLLOWS: FABRICATE A DISABLING SLUG OF CESIUM TRIPHENYL METHYL, ISOTOPE 137 OF CESIUM, OF 99% PURITY, TO BE USED. SLUG TO BE CYLINDRICAL 2.346 CM DIAMETER, 5.844 CM LENGTH. COMPONENTS OF SUBJECT DEVICE NOW IN LABORATORY TO BE REASSEMBLED TO THOSE REMAINING IN FIELD, WITH SLUG CONNECTED ELECTRICALLY AND MECHANICALLY ACROSS PROBE POINTS OUR NUMBER 11 AND OUR NUMBER 12A IN ARMING MECHANISM OF DEVICE. PRIME PROGRAMMED COMMAND OF DEVICE WILL THEN BE DISABLED FOR TIME EQUAL TO ONE HALF-LIFE OF ISOTOPE Cs-137 . . .

There were more details on how the "subject device" was to be disabled—he had forbidden his own computer to ever display or store in memory the word "berserker" in connection with any of his work. But Sabel did not read all the details at once. He was busy looking up the half-life of cesium-137. It turned out to be thirty years! Thirty standard years!

He had beaten it. He had won. Fists clenched, Sabel let out exultation in a great, private, and almost silent shout . . .

This instinctive caution was perhaps well-timed, for at once a chime announced a caller, at the door that led out to the mall. Sabel nervously wiped the displayed words from his computer screen. Might the girl have come back? Not because she had forgotten something—she had brought nothing with her but her clothes.

But instead of the girl's face, his video intercom showed him the deceptively jovial countenance of Chief Deputy Guardian Gunavarman. Had Sabel not become aware of the Potentate's presence on the Fortress, he might have had a bad moment at the sight. As matters stood, he felt prepared; and after a last precautionary glance around the lab, he let the man in confidently.

"Guardian. It is not often that I am honored by a visit from you."

"Doctor Sabel." The black-robed visitor respectfully returned the scientist's bow. "It is always a pleasure, when I can find the time. I wish my own work were always as interesting as yours must be. Well. You know of course that our esteemed Potentate is now in the Fortress . . ."

The discussion, on the necessity of being prepared for a VIP inspection, went just about as Sabel had expected. Gunavarman walked about as he spoke, eyes taking in the lab, their intelligence operating on yet a different level than either Sabel's or Greta Thamar's. The smiling lips asked Sabel just what, exactly, was he currently working on? What could he demonstrate, as dramatically as possible but safely of course, for the distinguished visitor?

Fortunately for Sabel he had been given a little advance time in which to think about these matters. He suggested now one or two things that might provide an impressive demonstration. "When must I have them ready?"

"Probably not sooner than two days from now, or more than five. You will be given advance notice of the exact time." But the Guardian, when Sabel pressed him, refused to commit himself on just how much advance notice would be given.

The real danger of this Potentate visit, thought Sabel as he saw his caller out, was that it was going to limit his mobility. A hurried field trip to the outer surface was going to be essential, to get incriminating materials out of his lab. Because he was sure that a security force of Guardians was going to descend on the place just before the Potentate appeared. More or less politely, but thoroughly, they would turn it inside out. There were those on every world of his dominion who for one reason or another wished the Potentate no good.

After a little thought, Sabel went to his computer terminal and punched in an order directed to the metallic fabrication machines in the Fortress's main workshops, an order for the disabling slug as specified by his computer. He knew well how the automated systems worked, and took care to place the order in such a way that no other human being would ever be presented with a record of it. The machines reported at once that delivery should take several hours.

The more he thought about it, the more essential it seemed for him to get the necessary field excursion out of the way as quickly as he could. Therefore while waiting for the slug to be delivered, he loaded up his flyer, with berserker parts hidden among tools in various containers. The vehicle was another thing that had been built to his special order. It was unusually small in all three dimensions, so he could drive it deeply into the caves and passages and cracks

of ancient battle-damage that honeycombed the outer
stonework of the Fortress.

A packet containing the slug he had ordered came
with a clack into his laboratory through the old-
fashioned pneumatic system still used for small deliv-
eries, direct from the workshops. Sabel's first look at
the cesium alloy startled him. A hard solid at room
temperature, the slug was red as blood inside a
statglass film evidently meant to protect it against
contamination and act as a radiation shield for human
handlers as well. He slid it into a pocket of his light
spacesuit, and was ready.

The lab locked up behind him, he sat in his flyer's
small open cab and exited the rooftop airlock in a
modest puff of fog. The air and moisture were mostly
driven back into recycling vents by the steady gravitic
pressure of the Radiant above. His flyer's small, silent engine worked against the curve of space that
the Radiant imposed, lifting him and carrying him on
a hand-controlled flight path that skimmed over glass-
roofed plazas and apartment complexes and offices.
In its concavity, the inner surface of the Fortress fell
more distant from his straight path, then reapproached.
Ahead lay the brightly lighted mouth of the traffic
shaft that would lead him out to the Fortress's outer
layers.

Under Sabel's briskly darting flyer there now passed
a garish, glassed-in amusement mall. There entertainment, sex, and various kinds of drugs were all for
sale. The *Contrat Rouge* he thought was somewhere
in it. He wondered in passing if the girl Greta understood that here her occupation put her very near the
bottom of the social scale, a small step above the
level of the barely tolerable prostitutes? Perhaps she
knew. Or when she found out, she would not greatly

care. She would probably be moving on, before very
long, to some world with more conventional mores.

Sabel had only vague ideas of how folk in the field
of popular entertainment lived. He wondered if he
might go sometime to watch her perform publicly. It
was doubtful that he would. To be seen much in the
Contrat Rouge could do harm to one in his position.

The wide mouth of the shaft engulfed his flyer. A
few other craft, electronically guided, moved on ahead
of his or flickered past. Strings of lights stretched
vertiginously down and ahead. The shaft was straight;
the Fortress had no appreciable rotation, and there
was no need to take coriolis forces into account in
traveling through it rapidly. With an expertise born
of his many repetitions of this flight, Sabel waited for
the precisely proper moment to take back full manual control. The gravitic pressure of the Radiant,
behind him and above, accelerated his passage steadily. He fell straight through the two kilometers' thick-
ness of stone and reinforcing beams that composed
most of the Fortress's bulk. The sides of the vast
shaft, now moving faster and faster past him, were
ribbed by the zig-zag joints of titanic interlocking
blocks.

This is still Dardania, here, he thought to himself, as usual at this point. The Earth-descended
Dardanians, who had built the Fortress and flour-
ished in it even before berserkers came to the human portion of the Galaxy, had wrought with awesome
energy, and a purpose not wholly clear to modern
eyes. The Fortress, after all, defended not much of
anything except the Radiant itself, which hardly
needed protection from humanity. Their engineers
must have tugged all the stone to build the Fort
through interstellar distances, at God alone knew

what expense of energy and time. Maybe Queen
Helen had let them know she would be pleased by
it, and that had been enough.

The Fortress contained about six hundred cubic
kilometers of stone and steel and enclosed space,
even without including the vast, clear central cavity.
Counting visitors and transients, there were now at
any moment approximately a hundred thousand human beings in residence. Their stores and parks and
dwellings and laboratories and shops occupied, for
the most part, only small portions of the inner surface, where gravity was normal and the light from
the Radiant was bright. From the outer surface,
nearby space was keenly watched by the sensors of
the largely automated defense system; there was a
patchy film of human activity there. The remainder
of the six hundred cubic kilometers were largely
desert now, honeycombed with cracks and designed
passages, spotted with still-undiscovered troves of
Dardanian tombs and artifacts, for decades almost
unexplored, virtually abandoned except by the few
who, like Sabel, researched the past.

Now he saw a routine warning begin to blink on
the small control panel of his flyer. Close ahead the
outer end of the transport shaft was yawning, and
through it he could see the stars. A continuation of
his present course would soon bring him into the
area surveyed by the defense system.

As his flyer emerged from the shaft, Sabel had the
stars beneath his feet, the bulk of the Fortress seemingly balanced overhead. With practiced skill he
turned now at right angles to the Radiant's force. His
flyer entered the marked notch of another traffic
lane, this one grooved into the Fortress's outer armored surface. The bulk of it remained over his head

and now seemed to rotate with his motion. Below him passed stars, while on the dark rims of the traffic lane to either side he caught glimpses of the anti-quated but still operational defensive works. Blunt snouts of missile-launchers, skeletal fingers of mass-drivers and beam-projectors, the lenses and screens and domes of sensors and field generators. All the hardware was still periodically tested, but in all his journeyings this way Sabel had never seen any of it looking anything but inactive. War had long ago gone elsewhere.

Other traffic, scanty all during his flight, had now vanished altogether. The lane he was following branched, and Sabel turned left, adhering to his usual route. If anyone should be watching him today, no deviation from his usual procedure would be ob-served. Not yet, anyway. Later . . . later he would make very sure that nobody was watching.

Here came a landmark on his right. Through an-other shaft piercing the Fortress a wand of the Radi-ant's light fell straight to the outer surface, where part of it was caught by the ruined framework of an auxiliary spaceport, long since closed. In that perma-nent radiance the old beams glowed like twisted night-flowers, catching at the light before it fell away to vanish invisibly and forever among the stars.

Just before he reached this unintended beacon, Sabel turned sharply again, switching on his bright running lights as he did so. Now he had entered a vast battle-crack in the stone and metal of the For-tress's surface, a dark uncharted wound that in Dardanian times had been partially repaired by a frail-looking spiderwork of metal beams. Familiar with the way, Sabel steered busily, choosing the proper passage amid obstacles. Now the stars were dropping out of view behind him. His route led him up again, into the lightless ruined passages where nothing seemed to have changed since Helen died.

Another minute of flight through twisting ways, some of them designed and others accidental. Then, obeying a sudden impulse, Sabel braked his flyer to a hovering halt. In the remote past this passage had been air-filled, the monumental length and breadth of it well suited for mass ceremony. Dardanian pictures and glyphs filled great portions of its long walls. Sabel had looked at them a hundred times before, but now he swung his suited figure out of the flyer's airless cab and walked close to the wall, moving buoyantly in the light gravity, as if to inspect them once again. This was an ideal spot to see if anyone was really following him. Not that he had any logical reason to think that someone was. But the feeling was strong that he could not afford to take a chance.

As often before, another feeling grew when he stood here in the silence and darkness that were broken only by his own presence and that of his machines. Helen herself was near. In Sabel's earlier years there had been something religious in this experience. Now . . . but it was still somehow comforting.

He waited, listening, thinking. Helen's was not the only presence near, of course. On three or four occasions at least during the past ten years (there might have been more that Sabel had never heard about) explorers had discovered substantial concentrations of berserker wreckage out in these almost abandoned regions. Each time Sabel had heard of such a find being reported to the Guardians, he had promptly petitioned them to be allowed to examine the materials, or at least to be shown a summary of whatever information the Guardians might manage to extract. His pleas had vanished into the bureaucratic maw. Gradually he had come to understand that they would never tell him anything about berserkers. The Guardians were jealous of his relative success and fame. Besides, their supposed job of protecting humanity on the Fortress now actually gave them almost nothing to do. A few newly-discovered berserker parts could be parlayed into endless hours of technical and administrative work. Just keeping secrets could be made into a job, and they were not about to share any secrets with outsiders.

But, once Sabel had become interested in berserkers as a possible source of data on the Radiant, he found ways to begin a study of them. His study was at first bookish and indirect, but it advanced; there was always more information available on a given subject than a censor realized, and a true scholar knew how to find it out.

And Sabel came also to distrust the Guardians' competence in the scholarly aspects of their own field. Even if they had finally agreed to share their findings with him, he thought their pick-axe methods unlikely to extract from a berserker's memory anything of value. They had refused of course to tell him what their methods were, but he could not imagine them doing anything imaginatively.

Secure in his own space helmet, he whispered now to himself: "If I want useful data from my own computer, I don't tear it apart. I communicate with it instead."

Cold silence and darkness around him, and nothing more. He remounted his flyer and drove on. Shortly he came to where the great corridor was

broken by a battle-damage crevice, barely wide enough
for his small vehicle, and he turned slowly, maneuvering his way in. Now he must go slowly, despite
the number of times that he had traveled this route
before. After several hundred meters of jockeying
his way along, his headlights picked up his semi-
permanent base camp structure in a widening of the
passageway ahead. It looked half bubble, half spider-
web, a tentlike thing whose walls hung slackly now
but were inflatable with atmosphere. Next to it he
had dug out of the stone wall a niche just big enough
to park his flyer in. The walls of the niche were
lightly marked now from his previous parkings. He
eased in now, set down gently, and cut power.

On this trip he was not going to bother to inflate
his shelter; he was not going to be out here long
enough to occupy it. Instead he began at once to
unload from the flyer what he needed, securing things
to his backpack as he took them down. The idea that
he was being followed now seemed so improbable
that he gave it no more thought. As soon as he had
all he wanted on his back, he set off on foot down
one of the branching crevices that radiated from the
nexus where he had placed his camp.

He paused once, after several meters, listening
intently. Not now for nonexistent spies who might
after all be following. For something active ahead.
Suppose it had, somehow, after all, got itself free
. . . but there was no possibility. He was carrying
most of its brain with him right now. Around him,
only the silence of ages, and the utter cold. The cold
could not pierce his suit. The silence, though . . .

The berserker was exactly as he had left it, days
ago. It was partially entombed, caught like some
giant mechanical insect in opaque amber. Elephant-

sized metal shoulders and a ruined head protruded from a bank of centuries-old slag. Fierce weaponry must have melted the rock, doubtless at the time of the Templars' reconquest of the Fortress, more than a hundred years ago.

Sabel when he came upon it for the first time understood at once that the berserker's brain might well still be functional. He knew too that there might be destructor devices still working, built into the berserker to prevent just such an analysis of captured units as he was suddenly determined to attempt. Yet he had nerved himself to go to work on the partially shattered braincase that protruded from the passage wall almost like a mounted trophy head. Looking back now, Sabel was somewhat aghast at the risks he had taken. But he had gone ahead. If there were any destructors, they had not fired. And it appeared to him now that he had won.

He took the cesium slug out of his pocket and put it into a tool that stripped it of statglass film and held it ready for the correct moment in the reconstruction process. And the reconstruction went smoothly and quickly, the whole process taking no more than minutes. Aside from the insertion of the slug it was mainly a matter of reconnecting subsystems and of attaching a portable power supply that Sabel now unhooked from his belt; it would give the berserker no more power than might be needed for memory and communication.

Yet, as soon as power was supplied, one of the thin limb stumps that protruded from the rock surface began to vibrate, with a syncopated buzzing. It must be trying to move.

Sabel had involuntarily backed up a step; yet reason told him that his enemy was effectively powerless to harm him. He approached again, and plugged a communications cord into a jack he had installed. When he spoke to it, it was in continuation of the dialogue in the laboratory.

"Now you are constrained, as you put it, to answer whatever questions I may ask." Whether it was going to answer truthfully or not was something he could not yet tell.

It now answered him in its own voice, cracked, queer, inhuman. "Now I am constrained."

Relief and triumph compounded were so strong that Sabel had to chuckle. The thing sounded so immutably certain of what it said, even as it had sounded certain saying the exact opposite back in the lab.

Balancing buoyantly on his toes in the light gravity, he asked it: "How long ago were you damaged, and stuck here in the rock?"

"My timers have been out of operation."

That sounded reasonable. "At some time before you were damaged, though, some visual observations of the Radiant probably became stored somehow in your memory banks. You know what I am talking about from our conversation in the laboratory. Remember that I will be able to extract useful information from even the most casual, incidental video records, provided they were made in Radiant light when you were active."

"I remember." And as the berserker spoke there came faintly to Sabel's ears a grinding, straining sound, conducted through his boots from somewhere under the chaotic surface of once-molten rock.

"What are you doing?" he demanded sharply. God knew what weapons it had been equipped with, what potential powers it still had.

Blandly the berserker answered: "Trying to re-establish function in my internal power supply."

"You will cease that effort at once! The supply I have connected is sufficient."

"Order acknowledged." And at once the grinding stopped.

Sabel fumbled around, having a hard time trying to make a simple connection with another small device that he removed from his suit's belt. If only he did not tend to sweat so much. "Now. I have here a recorder. You will play into it all the video records you have that might be useful to me in my research on the Radiant's spectrum. Do not erase any records from your own banks. I may want to get at them again later."

"Order acknowledged." In exactly the same cracked tones as before.

Sabel got the connection made at last. Then he crouched there, waiting for what seemed endless time, until his recorder signalled that the data flow had ceased.

And back in his lab, hours later, Sabel sat glaring destruction at the inoffensive stonework of the wall. His gaze was angled downward, in the direction of his unseen opponent, as if his anger could pierce and blast through the kilometers of rock.

The recorder had been filled with garbage. With nonsense. Virtually no better than noise. His own computer was still trying to unscramble the hopeless mess, but it seemed the enemy had succeeded in . . . still, perhaps it had not been a ploy of the berserker's at all. Only, perhaps, some kind of trouble with the coupling of the recorder input to . . .

He had, he remembered distinctly, told the berserker what the input requirements of the recorder were. But he had not explicitly ordered it to meet them. And he could not remember that it had ever said it would.

Bad, Sabel. A bad mistake to make in dealing with any kind of a machine. With a berserker . . .

A communicator made a melodious sound. A moment later, its screen brought Guardian Gunavarman's face and voice into the lab.

"Dr. Sabel, will your laboratory be in shape for a personal inspection by the Potentate three hours from now?"

"I—I—yes, it will. In fact, I will be most honored," he remembered to add, in afterthought.

"Good. Excellent. You may expect the security party a few minutes before that time."

As soon as the connection had been broken, Sabel looked around. He was in fact almost ready to be inspected. Some innocuous experiments were in place to be looked at and discussed. Almost everything that might possibly be incriminating had been got out of the way. Everything, in fact, except . . . he pulled the small recorder cartridge from his computer and juggled it briefly in his hand. The chance was doubtless small that any of his impending visitors would examine or play the cartridge, and smaller still that they might recognize the source of information on it if they did. Yet in Sabel's heart of hearts he was not so sure that the Guardians could be depended upon to be incompetent. And there was no reason for him to take even a small chance. There were, there had to be, a thousand public places where one might secrete an object as small as this. Where no one would notice it until it was retrieved

. . . there were of course the public storage facilities, on the far side of the Fortress, near the spaceport.

To get to any point in the Fortress served by the public transportation network took only a few minutes. He had to switch from moving slidewalk to high-speed elevator in a plaza that fronted on the entertainment district, and as he crossed the plaza his eye was caught by a glowing red sign a hundred meters or so down the mall: *Contrat Rouge*.

His phantom followers were at his back again, and to try to make them vanish he passed the elevator entrance as if that had not been his goal at all. He was not wearing his blue habit today, and as he entered the entertainment mall none of the few people who were about seemed to take notice of him.

A notice board outside the *Contrat Rouge* informed Sabel in glowing letters that the next scheduled dance performance was several hours away. It might be expected that he would know that, had he really started out with the goal of seeing her perform. Sabel turned and looked around, trying to decide what to do next. There were not many people in sight. But too many for him to decide if any of them might really have been following him.

Now the doorman was starting to take notice of him. So Sabel approached the man, clearing his throat. "I was looking for Greta Thamar?"

Tall and with a bitter face, the attendant looked as Sabel imagined a policeman ought to look. "Girls aren't in yet."

"She lives somewhere nearby, though?"

"Try public info."

And perhaps the man was somewhat surprised to see that that was what Sabel, going to a nearby booth, actually did next. The automated information service unhesitatingly printed out Greta's address listing for him, and Sabel was momentarily surprised: he had pictured her as beseiged by men who saw her on stage, having to struggle for even a minimum of privacy. But then he saw a stage name printed out in parentheses beside her own; those inquiring for her under the stage name would doubtless be given no information except perhaps the time of the next performance. And the doorman? He doubtless gave the same two answers to the same two questions a dozen times a day, and made no effort to keep track of names.

As Sabel had surmised, the apartment was not far away. It looked quite modest from the outside. A girl's voice, not Greta's, answered when he spoke into the intercom at the door. He felt irritated that they were probably not going to be able to be alone.

A moment later the door opened. Improbable blond hair framed a face of lovely ebony above a dancer's body. "I'm Greta's new roommate. She ought to be back in a few minutes." The girl gave Sabel an almost-amused appraisal. "I was just going out myself. But you can come in and wait for her if you like."

"I . . . yes, thank you." Whatever happened, he wouldn't be able to stay long. He had to leave himself plenty of time to get rid of the recorder cartridge somewhere and get back to the lab. But certainly there were at least a few minutes to spare.

He watched the blond dancer out of sight. Sometime, perhaps . . . Then, left alone, he turned to a half-shaded window through which he could see a large part of the nearby plaza. Still there was no one in sight who looked to Sabel as if they might be following him. He moved from the window to stand

in front of a cheap table. If he left before seeing
Greta, should he leave her a note? And what ought
he to say?

His personal communicator beeped at his belt.
When he raised it to his face he found Chief Deputy
Gunavarman looking out at him from the tiny screen.

"Doctor Sabel, I had expected you would be in
your laboratory now. Please get back to it as soon as
possible; the Potentate's visit has been moved up by
about two hours. Where are you now?"

"I . . . ah . . ." *What might be visible in Gunavarman's screen?* "The entertainment district."

The chronic appearance of good humor in the
Guardian's face underwent a subtle shift; perhaps
now there was something of genuine amusement in
it. "It shouldn't take you long to get back, then.
Please hurry. Shall I send an escort?"

"No. Not necessary. Yes. At once." Then they
were waiting for him at the lab. It was even possible
that they could meet him right outside this apartment's door. As Sabel reholstered his communicator,
he looked around him with quick calculation. There.
Low down on one wall was a small ventilation grill of
plastic, not much broader than his open hand. It was
a type in common use within the Fortress. Sabel
crouched down. The plastic bent springily in his
strong fingers, easing out of its socket. He slid the
recorder into the dark space behind, remembering
to wipe it free of fingerprints first.

The Potentate's visit to the lab went well. It took
longer than Sabel had expected, and he was com-
plimented on his work, at least some of which the
great leader seemed to understand. It wasn't until
next morning, when Sabel was wondering how soon

he ought to call on Greta again, that he heard during a chance encounter with a colleague that some unnamed young woman in the entertainment district had been arrested.

Possession of a restricted device, that was the charge. The first such arrest in years, and though no official announcement had yet been made, the Fortress was buzzing with the event, probably in several versions. The wording of the charge meant that the accused was at least suspected of actual contact with a berserker; it was the same one, technically, that would have been placed against Sabel if his secret activities had been discovered. And it was the more serious form of goodlife activity, the less serious consisting in forming clubs or cells of conspiracy, of sympathy to the enemy, perhaps having no real contact with berserkers.

Always in the past when he had heard of the recovery of any sort of berserker hardware, Sabel had called Gunavarman, to ask to be allowed to take part in the investigation. He dared not make an exception this time.

"Yes, Doctor," said the Guardian's voice from a small screen. "A restricted device is in our hands today. Why do you ask?"

"I think I have explained my interest often enough in the past. If there is any chance that this—device— contains information pertinent to my studies, I should like to apply through whatever channels may be necessary—"

"Perhaps I can save you the trouble. This time the device is merely the storage cartridge of a video recorder of a common type. It was recovered last night during a routine search of some newcomers' quarters in the entertainment district. The information on the recorder is intricately coded and we haven't solved it yet. But I doubt it has any connection with cosmophysics. This is just for your private information of course."

"Of course. But—excuse me—if you haven't broken the code why do you think this device falls into the restricted category?"

"There is a certain signature, shall we say, in the coding process. Our experts have determined that the information was stored at some stage in a berserker's memory banks. One of the two young women who lived in the apartment committed suicide before she could be questioned—a typical goodlife easy-out, it appears. The other suspect so far denies everything. We're in the process of obtaining a court order for some M-E, and that'll take care of that."

"Memory extraction. I didn't know that you could still—?"

"Oh, yes. Though nowadays there's a formal legal procedure. The questioning must be done in the presence of official witnesses. And if innocence of the specific charge is established, questioning must be halted. But in this case I think we'll have no trouble."

Sabel privately ordered a printout of all court documents handled during the previous twenty-four hours. There it was: Greta Thamar, order for memory-extraction granted. At least she was not dead.

To try to do anything for her would of course have been completely pointless. If the memory-extraction worked to show her guilt, it should show also that he, Sabel, was only an innocent chance acquaintance. But in fact it must work to show her innocence, and then she would be released. She would regain her full mental faculties in time—enough of them, anyway, to be a dancer.

Why, though, had her roommate killed herself? Entertainers. Unstable people . . .

Even if the authorities should someday learn that he had known Greta Thamar, there was no reason for him to come forward today and say so. No; he wasn't supposed to know as yet that she was the one arrested. Gunavarman had mentioned no names to him.

No, indeed, the best he could hope for by getting involved would be entanglement in a tedious, time-wasting investigation. Actually of course he would be risking much worse than that.

Actually it was his work, the extraction of scientific truth, that really mattered, not he. And, certainly, not one little dancer more or less. But if he went, his work went too. Who else was going to extract from the Templar Radiant the truths that would open shining new vistas of cosmophysics? Only seven other Radiants were known to exist in the entire Galaxy. None of the others were as accessible to study as this one was, and no one knew this one nearly as well as Georgicus Sabel knew it.

Yes, it would be pointless indeed for him to try to do anything for the poor girl. But he was surprised to find himself going through moments in which he felt that he was going to have to try.

Meanwhile, if there were even the faintest suspicion of him, if the Guardians were watching his movements, then an abrupt cessation of his field trips would be more likely to cause trouble than their continuation. And, once out in the lonely reaches of Dardania, he felt confident of being able to tell whether the Guardians were following him or not.

This time he took with him a small hologramstage, so he could look at the video records before he brought them back.

"This time," he said to the armored braincase projecting from the slag-bank, "you are ordered to give me the information in intelligible form."

Something in its tremendous shoulders buzzed, a syncopated vibration. "Order acknowledged."

And what he had been asking for was shown to him at last. Scene after scene, made in natural Radiantlight. Somewhere on the inner surface of the Fortress, surrounded by smashed Dardanian glass roofs, a row of berserkers stood as if for inspection by some commanding machine. Yes, he should definitely be able to get something out of that. And out of this one, a quite similar scene. And out of—

"Wait. Just a moment. Go back, let me see that one again. What was that?"

He was once more looking at the Fortress's inner surface, bathed by the Radiant's light. But this time no berserkers were visible. The scene was centered on a young woman, who wore space garb of a design unfamiliar to Sabel. It was a light-looking garment that did not much restrict her movements, and the two-second segment of recording showed her in the act of performing some gesture. She raised her arms to the light above as if in the midst of some rite or dance centered on the Radiant itself. Her dark hair, short and curly, bore a jeweled diadem. Her longlashed eyes were closed, in a face of surpassing loveliness.

He watched it three more times. "Now wait again. Hold the rest of the records. Who was that?"

To a machine, a berserker, all human questions and answers were perhaps of equal unimportance. Its voice gave the same tones to them all. It said to Sabel: "The life-unit Helen Dardan."

"But—" Sabel had a feeling of unreality. "Show it once more, and stop the motion right in the middle— yes, that's it. Now, how old is this record?"

"It is of the epoch of the 451st century, in your time-coordinate system."

"Before berserkers came to the Fortress? And why do you tell me it is she?"

"It is a record of Helen Dardan. No other existed. I was given it to use as a means of identification. I am a specialized assassin-machine and was sent on my last mission to destroy her."

"You—you claim to be the machine that actually— actually killed Helen Dardan?"

"No."

"Then explain."

"With other machines, I was programmed to kill her. But I was damaged and trapped here before the mission could be completed."

Sabel signed disagreement. By now he felt quite sure that the thing could see him somehow. "You were trapped during the Templars' reconquest. That's when this molten rock must have been formed. Well after the time when Helen lived."

"That is when I was trapped. But only within an hour of the Templars' attack did we learn where the life-unit Helen Dardan had been hidden, in suspended animation."

"The Dardanians hid her from you somehow, and you couldn't find her until then?"

"The Dardanians hid her. I do not know whether she was ever found or not."

Sabel tried to digest this. "You're saying that for all you know, she might be still entombed somewhere, in suspended animation—and still alive."

"Confirm."

He looked at his video recorder. For a moment he could not recall why he had brought it here. "Just where was this hiding place of hers supposed to be?"

As it turned out, after Sabel had struggled through a translation of the berserkers' coordinate system into his own, the supposed hiding place was not far away at all. Once he had the location pinpointed it took him only minutes to get to the described intersection of Dardanian passageways. There, according to his informant, Helen's life-support coffin had been mortared up behind a certain obscure marking on a wall.

This region was free of the small blaze-marks that Sabel himself habitually put on the walls to remind himself of what ground he had already covered in his systematic program of exploration. And it was a region of some danger, perhaps, for here in relatively recent times there had been an extensive crumbling of stonework. What had been an intersection of passages had become a rough cave, piled high with pieces great and small of what had been wall and floor and overhead. The fragments were broken and rounded to some extent, sharp corners knocked away. Probably at intervals they did a stately mill-dance in the low gravity, under some perturbation of the Fortress's stately secular movement round the Radiant in space. Eventually the fallen fragments would probably grind themselves into gravel, and slide away to accumulate in low spots in the nearby passages.

But today they still formed a rough, high mound.

Sabel with his suit lights could discern a dull egg-shape nine-tenths buried in this mound. It was rounder and smoother than the broken masonry, and the size of a piano or a little larger.

He clambered toward it, and without much trouble succeeded in getting it almost clear of rock. It was made of some tough, artificial substance; and in imagination he could fit into it any of the several types of suspended-animation equipment that he had seen.

What now? Suppose, just suppose, that any real chance existed . . . he dared not try to open up the thing here in the airless cold. Nor had he any tools with him at the moment that would let him try to probe the inside gently. He had to go back to base camp and get the flyer here somehow.

Maneuvering his vehicle to his find proved easier than he had feared. He found a roundabout way to reach the place, and in less than an hour had the ovoid secured to his flyer with adhesive straps. Hauling it slowly back to base camp, he reflected that whatever was inside was going to have to remain secret, for a while at least. The announcement of any important find would bring investigators swarming out here. And that Sabel could not afford, until every trace of the berserker's existence had been erased.

Some expansion of the tent's fabric was necessary before he could get the ovoid in, and leave himself with space to work. Once he had it in a securely air-filled space, he put a gentle heater to work on its outer surface, to make it easier to handle. Then he went to work with an audio pickup to see what he could learn of the interior.

There was activity of some kind inside, that much was obvious at once. The sounds of gentle machinery, which he supposed might have been started by his disturbance of the thing, or by the presence of warm air around it now.

Subtle machinery at work. And then another sound, quite regular. It took Sabel's memory a little time to match it with the cadence of a living human heart.

He had forgotten about time, but in fact not much time had passed before he considered that he was ready for the next step. The outer casing opened for him easily. Inside, he confronted great complexity; yes, obviously sophisticated life-support. And within that an interior shell, eyed with glass windows. Sabel shone in a light.

As usual in suspended-animation treatment, the occupant's skin had been covered with a webbed film of half-living stuff to help in preservation. But the film had torn away now from around the face.

And the surpassing beauty of that face left Sabel no room for doubt. Helen Dardan was breathing, and alive.

Might not all, all, be forgiven one who brought the Queen of Love herself to life? All, even goodlife work, the possession of restricted devices?

There was also to be considered, though, the case of a man who at a berserker's direction unearthed the Queen and thereby brought about her final death.

Of course an indecisive man, one afraid to take risks, would not be out here now faced with his problem. Sabel had already unslung his emergency medirobot, a thing the size of a suitcase, from its usual perch at the back of the flyer, and had it waiting inside the tent. Now, like a man plunging into deep, cold water, he fumbled open the fasteners of the interior shell, threw back its top, and quickly stretched probes from the medirobot to Helen's head and chest and wrist. He tore away handfuls of the half-living foam.

Even before he had the third probe connected, her dark eyes had opened and were looking at him. He thought he could see awareness and understanding in them. Her last hopes on being put to sleep must have been for an awakening no worse than this, at hands that might be strange but were not metal.

"Helen." Sabel could not help but feel that he was pretending, acting, when he spoke the name. "Can you hear me? Understand?" He spoke in Standard; the meagre store of Dardanian that he had acquired from ancient recordings having completely deserted him for the moment. But he thought a Dardanian aristocrat should know enough Standard to grasp his meaning and the language had not changed enormously in the centuries since her entombment.

"You're safe now," he assured her, on his space-suited knees beside her bed. When a flicker in her eyes seemed to indicate relief, he went on: "The berserkers have been driven away."

Her lips parted slightly. They were full and perfect. But she did not speak. She raised herself a little, and moved to bare a shoulder and an arm from clinging foam.

Nervously Sabel turned to the robot. If he was interpreting its indicators correctly, the patient was basically in quite good condition. To his not-really-expert eye the machine signalled that there were high drug levels in her bloodstream; high, but falling. Hardly surprising, in one just being roused from suspended animation.

"There's nothing to fear, Helen. Do you hear me?

The berserkers have been beaten." He didn't want to tell her, not right away at least, that glorious Dardania was no more.

She had attained almost a sitting position by now, leaning on the rich cushions of her couch. There was some relief in her eyes, yes, but uneasiness as well. And still she had not uttered a word.

As Sabel understood it, people awakened from SA ought to have some light nourishment at once. He hastened to offer food and water both. Helen sampled what he gave her, first hesitantly, then with evident enjoyment.

"Never mind, you don't have to speak to me right away. The-war-is-over." This last was in his best Dardanian, a few words of which were now belatedly willing to be recalled.

"You-are-Helen." At this he thought he saw agreement in her heavenly face. Back to Standard now. "I am Georgicus Sabel. Doctor of Cosmophysics, Master of . . . but what does all that matter to me, now? I have saved you. And that is all that counts."

She was smiling at him. And maybe after all this was a dream, no more . . .

More foam was peeling, clotted, from her skin. Good God, what was she going to wear? He bumbled around, came up with a spare coverall. Behind his turned back he heard her climbing from the cushioned container, putting the garment on.

What was this, clipped to his belt? The newly-charged video recorder, yes. It took him a little while to remember what he was doing with it. He must take it back to the lab, and make sure that the information on it was readable this time. After that, the berserker could be destroyed.

He already had with him in camp tools that could

break up metal, chemicals to dissolve it. But the berserker's armor would be resistant, to put it mildly. And it must be very thoroughly destroyed, along with the rock that held it, so that no one should ever guess it had existed. It would take time to do that. And special equipment and supplies, which Sabel would have to return to the city to obtain.

Three hours after she had wakened, Helen, dressed in a loose coverall, was sitting on cushions that Sabel had taken from her former couch and arranged on rock. She seemed content to simply sit and wait, watching her rescuer with flattering eyes, demanding nothing from him—except, as it soon turned out, his presence.

Painstakingly he kept trying to explain to her that he had important things to do, that he was going to have to go out, leave her here by herself for a time.

"I-must-go. I will come back. Soon." There was no question of taking her along, no matter what. At the moment there was only one spacesuit.

But, for whatever reason, she wouldn't let him go. With obvious alarm, and pleading gestures, she put herself in front of the airlock to bar his way.

"Helen. I really must. I—"

She signed disagreement, violently.

"But there is one berserker left, you see. We cannot be safe until it is—until—"

Helen was smiling at him, a smile of more than gratitude. And now Sabel could no longer persuade himself that this was not a dream. With a sinuous movement of unmistakable invitation, the Queen of Love was holding out her arms . . .

* * *

When he was thinking clearly and coolly once again, Sabel began again with patient explanations. "Helen. My darling. You see, I *must* go. To the city. To get some—"

A great light of understanding, acquiescence, dawned in her lovely face.

"There are some things I need, vitally. Then I swear I'll come right back. Right straight back here. You want me to bring someone with me, is that it? I—"

He was about to explain that he couldn't do that just yet, but her renewed alarm indicated that that was the last thing she would ask.

"All right, then. Fine. No one. I will bring a spare spacesuit . . . but that you are here will be my secret, our secret, for a while. Does that please you? Ah, my Queen!"

At the joy he saw in Helen's face, Sabel threw himself down to kiss her foot. "Mine alone!"

He was putting on his helmet now. "I will return in less than a day. If possible. The chronometer is over here, you see? But if I should be longer than a day, don't worry. There's everything you'll need, here in the shelter. I'll do my best to hurry."

Her eyes blessed him.

He had to turn back from the middle of the airlock, to pick up his video recording, almost forgotten.

How, when it came time at last to take the Queen into the city, was he going to explain his long concealment of her? She was bound to tell others how many days she had been in that far tent. Somehow there had to be a way around that problem. At the moment, though, he did not want to think about it. The Queen was his alone, and no one . . . but first, before anything else, the berserker had to be got rid of. No, before that even, he must see if its video data was good this time.

Maybe Helen knew, Helen could tell him, where cached Dardanian treasure was waiting to be found . . .

And she had taken him as lover, as casual bed-partner rather. Was that the truth of the private life and character of the great Queen, the symbol of chastity and honor and dedication to her people? Then no one, in the long run, would thank him for bringing her back to them.

Trying to think ahead, Sabel could feel his life knotting into a singularity at no great distance in the future. Impossible to try to predict what lay beyond. It was worse than uncertain; it was opaque.

This time his laboratory computer made no fuss about accepting the video records. It began to process them at once.

At his private information station Sabel called for a printout of any official news announcements made by the Guardians or the city fathers during the time he had been gone. He learned that the entertainer Greta Thamar had been released under the guardianship of her court-appointed lawyer, after memory extraction. She was now in satisfactory condition in the civilian wing of the hospital.

There was nothing else in the news about goodlife, or berserkers. And there had been no black-robed Guardians at Sabel's door when he came in.

DATING ANOMALY PRESENT was on the screen of Sabel's laboratory computer the next time he looked at it.

"Give details," he commanded.

RECORD GIVEN AS EPOCH 451st CENTURY
IDENTIFIES WITH SPECTRUM OF RADIANT
EPOCH 456th CENTURY, YEAR 23, DAY 152.

"Let me see."

It was, as some part of Sabel's mind already seemed
to know, the segment that showed Helen on the
inner surface of the Fortress, raising her arms ecstat-
ically as in some strange rite. Or dance.

The singularity in his future was hurtling toward
him quickly now. "You say—you say that the spectrum in this record is identical with the one we
recorded—what did you say? How long ago?"

38 DAYS 11 HOURS, APPROXIMATELY 44
MINUTES.

As soon as he had the destructive materials he
needed loaded aboard the flyer, he headed at top
speed back to base camp. He did not wait to obtain a
spare spacesuit.

Inside the tent, things were disarranged, as if Helen
perhaps had been searching restlessly for something.
Under the loose coverall her breast rose and fell
rapidly, as if she had recently been working hard, or
were in the grip of some intense emotion.

She held out her arms to him, and put on a glitter-
ing smile.

Sabel stopped just inside the airlock. He pulled
his helmet off and faced her grimly. "Who are you?"
he demanded.

She winced, and tilted her head, but would not
speak. She still held out her arms, and the glassy
smile was still in place.

"*Who are you, I said?* That hologram was made
just thirty-eight days ago."

Helen's face altered. The practiced expression was

still fixed on it, but now a different light played on her features. The light came from outside the shelter, and it was moving toward them.

There were four people out there, some with hand weapons leveled in Sabel's direction. Through the plastic he could not tell at once if their suited figures were those of men or women. Two of them immediately came in through the airlock, while the other two remained outside, looking at the cargo Sabel had brought out on the flyer.

"God damn, it took you long enough." Helen's lovely lips had formed some words at last.

The man who entered first, gun drawn, ignored Sabel for the moment and inspected her with a sour grin. "I see you came through five days in the cooler in good shape."

"Easier than one day here with him—God damn." Helen's smile at Sabel had turned into an equally practiced snarl.

The second man to enter the shelter stopped just inside the airlock. He stood there with a hand on the gun holstered at his belt, watching Sabel alertly.

The first man now confidently holstered his weapon too, and concentrated his attention on Sabel. He was tall and bitter-faced, but he was no policeman. "I'm going to want to take a look inside your lab, and maybe get some things out. So hand over the key, or tell me the combination."

Sabel moistened his lips. "Who are you?" The words were not frightened, they were imperious with rage. "And who is this woman here?"

"I advise you to control yourself. She's been entertaining you, keeping you out of our way while we got a little surprise ready for the city. We each of us serve the Master in our own way . . . even you have already served. You provided the Master with enough power to call on us for help, some days ago . . . yes, what?" Inside this helmet he turned his head to look outside the shelter. "Out completely? Under its own power now? Excellent!"

He faced back toward Sabel. "And who am I? Someone who will get the key to your laboratory from you, one way or another, you may be sure. We've been working on you a long time already, many days. We saw to it that poor Greta got a new roommate, as soon as you took up with her. Poor Greta never knew . . . you see, we thought we might need your flyer and this final cargo of tools and chemicals to get the Master out. As it turned out, we didn't."

Helen, the woman Sabel had known as Helen, walked into his field of vision, turned her face to him as if to deliver a final taunt.

What it might have been, he never knew. Her dark eyes widened, in a parody of fainting fright. In the next moment she was slumping to the ground.

Sabel had a glimpse of the other, suited figures tumbling. Then a great soundless, invisible, cushioned club smote at his whole body. The impact had no direction, but there was no way to stand against it. His muscles quit on him, his nerves dissolved. The rocky ground beneath the shelter came up to catch his awkward fall with bruising force.

Once down, it was impossible to move a hand or foot. He had to concentrate on simply trying to breathe.

Presently he heard the airlock's cycling sigh. To lift his head and look was more than he could do; in his field of vision there were only suited bodies, and the ground.

Black boots, Guardian boots, trod to a halt close before his eyes. A hand gripped Sabel's shoulder and turned him part way up. Gunavarman's jovial eyes looked down at him for a triumphal moment ᐩbefore the Chief Deputy moved on.

Other black boots shuffled about. "Yes, this one's Helen Nadrad, all right—that's the name she used whoring at the Parisian Alley, anyway. I expect we can come up with another name or two for her if we look offworld. Ready to talk to us, Helen? Not yet? You'll be all right. Stunner wears off in an hour or so."

"Chief, I wonder what they expected to do with suspended animation gear? Well, we'll find out."

Gunavarman now began a radio conference with some distant personage. Sabel, in his agony of trying to breathe, to move, to speak, could hear only snatches of the talk:

"Holding meetings out here for some time, evidently . . . mining for berserker parts, probably . . . equipment . . . yes, Sire, the berserker recording was found in his laboratory this time . . . a publicity hologram of Helen Nadrad included in it, for some reason . . . yes, very shocking. But no doubt . . . we followed him out here just now. Joro, that's the goodlife organizer we've been watching, is here . . . yes, Sire. Thank you very much. I will pass on your remarks to my people here."

In a moment more the radio conversation had been concluded. Gunavarman, in glowing triumph, was bending over Sabel once again. "Prize catch," the Guardian murmured. "Something you'd like to say to me?"

Sabel was staring at the collapsed figure of Joro. Inside an imperfectly closed pocket of the man's space-

suit he could see a small, blood-red cylinder, a stub
of cut wire protruding from one end.

"Anything important, Doctor?"

He tried, as never before. Only a few words.
"Dr-aw . . . your . . . wea-pons . . ."

Gunavarman glanced round at his people swarming outside the tent. He looked confidently amused.
"Why?"

Now through the rock beneath the groundsheet of
his shelter Sabel could hear a subtly syncopated,
buzzing vibration, drawing near.

"Draw . . . your . . ."

Not that he really thought the little handguns were
likely to do them any good.

The instruments of science do not in themselves discover truth. And there are searchings that are not concluded by the coincidence of a pointer and a mark.

STARSONG

Forcing the passage through the dark nebula Taynarus cost them three fighting ships, and after that they took the casualties of a three-day battle as their boarding parties fought their way into Hell. The Battle Commander of the task force feared from the beginning to the end of the action that the computer in command on the berserker side would destroy the place and the living invaders with it, in a last *gotterdammerung* of destructor charges. But he could hope that the damped-field projectors his men took with him into the fight would prevent any nuclear explosion. He sent living men to board because it was believed that Hell held living human prisoners. His hopes were justified; or at least, for whatever reason, no nuclear explosion came.

The beliefs about prisoners were not easily confirmed. Ercul, the cybernetic psychologist who came to investigate when the fighting was over, certainly found humans there. In a way. In part. Odd organs that functioned in a sort-of way, interconnected with the non-human and the non-alive. The organs were most of them human brains, which had been grown in culture through use of the techniques that berserkers must have captured with some of our hospital ships.

137

Our human laboratories grow the culture-brains from seedlings of human embryo-tissue, grow them to adult size and then dissect them as needed. A doctor slices off a prefrontal lobe, say, and puts it into the skull of a man whose own corresponding brain-part has been destroyed by some disease or violence. The culture-brain material serves as a matrix for regrowth, raw material on which the old personality can reimpress itself. The culture-brains, raised in glass jars, are not human except in potential. Even a layman can readily distinguish one of them from a normally developed brain by the visible absence of the finer surface convolutions. The culture-brains cannot be human in the sense of maintaining sentient human minds. Certain hormones and other subtle chemicals of the body-environment are necessary for the development of a brain with personality—not to mention the need for the stimuli of experience, the continual impact of the senses. Indeed some sensory input is needed if the culture-brain is to develop even to the stage of a template usable by the surgeon. For this input music is commonly employed.

The berserkers had doubtless learned to culture livers and hearts and gonads as well as brains, but it was only man's thinking ability that interested them deeply. The berserkers must have stood in their computer-analogue of awe as they regarded the memory-capacity and the decision-making power that nature in a few billion years of evolution had managed to pack into the few hundred cubic centimeters of the human nervous system.

Off and on through their long war with men the berserkers had tried to incorporate human brains into their own circuitry. Never had they succeeded to their own satisfaction, but they kept trying.

The berserkers themselves of course named nothing. But men were not far wrong in calling this center of their research Hell. This Hell lay hidden in the center of the dark Taynarus nebula, which in turn was roughly centered in a triangle formed by the Zitz and Toxx and Yaty systems. Men had known for years what Hell was, and approximately where it was, before they could muster armed strength enough in this part of their sector of the galaxy to go in and find it and root it out.

"I certify that in this container there is no human life," said the cybernetic psychologist, Ercul, under his breath, at the same time stamping the words on the glassite case before him. Ercul's assistant gestured, and the able-bodied spaceman working with them pulled the power-connectors loose and let the thing in the tank begin to die. This one was not a culture-brain but had once been the nervous system of a living prisoner. It had been greatly damaged not only by removal of most of its human body but by being connected to a mass of electronic and micromechanical gear. Through some training program, probably a combination of punishment and reward, the berserker had then taught this brain to perform certain computing operations at great speed and with low probability of error. It seemed that every time the computations had been finished the mechanism in the case with the brain had immediately reset all the counters to zero and once more presented the same inputs, whereupon the brain's task had started over. The brain now seemed incapable of anything but going on with the job; and if that was really a kind of human life, which was not a possibility that Ercul was going to admit out loud, it was in his opinion a kind that was better terminated as soon as possible.

"Next case?" he asked the spacemen. Then he realized he had just made a horrible pun upon his judge's role. But none of his fellow harrowers of Hell seemed to have noticed it. But just give us a few more days on the job, he thought, and we will start finding things to laugh at.

Anyway, he had to get on with his task of trying to distinguish rescued prisoners—two of these had been confirmed so far, and might some day again look human—from collection of bottled though more or less functioning organs.

When they brought the next case before him, he had a bad moment, bad even for this day, recognizing some of his own work.

The story of it had started more than a standard year before, on the not-far-off planet of Zitz, in a huge hall that had been decorated and thronged for one of the merriest of occasions.

"Happy, honey?" Ordell Callison asked his bride, having a moment to take her hand and speak to her under the tumult of the wedding feast. It was not that he had any doubt of her happiness; it was just that the banal two-word question was the best utterance that he could find—unless, of course, he was to sing.

"Ohhh, happy, yes!" At the moment Eury was no more articulate than he. But the truth of her words was in her voice and in her eyes, marvelous as some song that Ordell might have made and sung.

Of course he was not going to be allowed to get away, even for his honeymoon, without singing one song at least.

"Sing something, Ordell!" That was Hyman Bolf, calling from across the vast banquet table, where he stood filling his cup at the crystal punch-fountain. The famed multifaith revivalist had come from Yaty system to perform the wedding ceremony. On landing, his private ship had misbehaved oddly, the hydrogen power lamp flaring so that the smoke of burnt insulation had caused the reverend to emerge from his cabin weeping with irritated eyes; but after that bad omen, everything had gone well for the rest of the day.

Other voices took it up at once. "Sing, Ordell!"

"Yes, you've got to. Sing!"

"But it's m'own wedding, and I don't feel quite right—"

His objections were overwhelmingly shouted down.

The man was music, and indeed his happiness today was such that he felt he might burst if he could not express it. He got to his feet, and one of his most trusted manservants, who had foreseen that Ordell would sing, was ready to bring him his self-invented instrument. Crammed into a small box that Ordell could hang from his neck like an accordion were a speaker system from woofer to tweet, plus a good bit of electronics and audionics; on the box's plain surface there were ten spots for Ordell's ten fingers to play upon. His music-box, he called it, having to call it something. Ordell's imitators had had bigger and flashier and better music-boxes made for them; but surprisingly few people, even among girls between twelve and twenty, cared to listen to Ordell's imitators.

So Ordell Callison sang at his own wedding, and his audience was enthralled by him as people always were; as people had been by no other performer in all the ancient records of Man. The highbrowed mu-

sic critics sat rapt in their places of honor at the head
table; the cultured and not-so-cultured moneyed folk
of Zitz and Toxx and Yaty, some of whom had come
in their private racing ships, and the more ordinary
guests, all were made happy by his song as no wine
could have made them. And the adolescent girls, the
Ordell fans who crowded and huddled inevitably
outside the doors, they yielded themselves to his
music to the point of fainting and beyond.

A couple of weeks later Ordell and Eury and his
new friends of the last fast years, the years of success
and staggering wealth, were out in space in their
sporty one-seater ships playing the game they called
Tag. This time Ordell was playing the game in a sort
of reversed way, dodging about in one corner of the
reserved volume of space, really trying to avoid the
girl-ships that fluttered past instead of going after
them.

He had been keeping one eye out for Eury's ship,
and getting a little anxious about not being able to
find it, when from out of nowhere there came shooting toward Ordell another boy-ship, the signals of
emergency blazing from it across the spectrum. In
another minute everyone had ceased to play. The
screens of all the little ships imaged the face of Arty,
the young man whose racer had just braked to a halt
beside Ordell's.

Arty was babbling: "I tried, Ordell—I mean I didn't
try to—I didn't mean her any harm—they'll get her
back—it wasn't my fault she—"

With what seemed great slowness, the truth of
what had happened became clear. Arty had chased
and overtaken Eury's ship, as was the way of the
game. He had clamped his ship to hers and boarded,

and then thought to claim the usual prize. But Eury
of course was married now, and being married meant
much to her, as it did to Ordell who today had only
played at catching girls. Somehow both of them had
thought that everyone else must see how the world
had changed since they were married, how the rules
of the game of Tag would have to be amended for
them from now on.

Unable to convince Arty by argument of how things
stood, Eury had had to struggle to make her point.
She had somehow injured her foot, trying to evade
him in the little cabin. He kept on stubbornly trying
to claim his prize. It came out later that he had only
agreed to go back to his own ship for a first aid kit
(she swore that her ship's kit was missing) after her
seeming promise that he could have what he wanted
when he returned.

But when he had gone back to his ship, she broke
her own racer free and fled. And he pursued. Drove
her into a corner, against the boundary of the safety
zone, which was guarded by automated warships
against the possibility of berserker incursions.

To get away from Arty she crossed that border in a
great speeding curve, no doubt meaning to come
back to safety within ten thousand miles or so.

She never made it. As her little racer sped close to
an outlying wisp of dark Taynarus, the berserker
machine that had been lurking there pounced out.

Of course Ordell did not hear the story in such
coherent form, but what he heard was enough. On
the screens of the other little ships his face at first
seemed to be turned to stone by what he heard; but
then his look became suddenly wild and mad. Arty
cringed away, but Ordell did not stop a moment for

him. Instead he drove at racer's speed out where his wife had gone. He shot through the zone of the protective patrols (which were set to keep intruders out, not to hold the mad or reckless in) and plunged between outlying dustclouds to enter one of the vast crevices that led into the heart of Taynarus; into the maze where ships and machines must all go slow, and from which no living human had emerged since the establishment of Hell.

Some hours later the outer sentries of the berserker came around his little ship, demanding in their well-learned human speech that he halt and submit to capture. He only slowed his little ship still further and began to sing to the berserker over the radio, taking his hands from his racer's controls to put his fingers on the keys of his music-box. Unsteered, his ship drifted away from the center of the navigable passage, grazing the nebular wall and suffering the pocking blasts of microcollisions with its gas and dust.

But before his ship was wrecked, the berserker's sentry-devices gave up shouting radio commands and sent a boarding party of machines.

Through the memory banks of Hell they had some experience of insanity, of the more bizarre forms of human behavior. They searched the racer for weapons, searched Ordell—allowed him to keep his music-box when it too had been examined and he kept on struggling for it—and passed him on as a prisoner to the jurisdiction of the inner guards.

Hell, a mass of fortified metal miles in diameter, received him and his racer through its main entrance. He got out of his ship and found himself able to breathe and walk and see where he was going; the physical environment in Hell was for the most part mild and pleasant, because prisoners did not as a rule survive very long, and the computer-brains of the berserker did not want to impose unnecessary stresses upon them.

The berserker devices having immediate control over the routine operations in Hell were themselves in large part organic, containing culture-brains grown for the purpose and some re-educated captured brains as well. These were all examples of the berserker's highest achievements in its attempts at reverse cybernation.

Before Ordell had taken a dozen steps away from his ship, he was stopped and questioned by one of these monsters. Half steel and circuitry, half culture-flesh, it carried in three crystal globes its three potentially-human brains, their too-smooth surfaces bathed in nutrient and woven with hair-fine wires.

"Why have you come here?" the monster asked him, speaking through a diaphragm in its midsection.

Only now did Ordell begin at all to make a conscious plan. At the core of his thought was the knowledge that in the human laboratories music was used to tune and tone the culture-brains, and that his own music was as superior for that purpose as it was by all other standards.

To the three-headed monster he sang very simply that he had come here only to seek his young wife, pure accident had brought her, ahead of time, to the end of her life. In one of the old formal languages in which he sang so well of deep things, he implored the power in charge of this domain of terror, this kingdom of silence and unborn creatures, to tie fast again the thread of Eury's life. If you deny me this, he sang, I cannot return to the world of the living alone, and you here will have us both.

The music, that had conveyed nothing but its mathematical elements to the cold computer-brains outside, melted the trained purpose of the inner, half-fleshly guardians. The three-brained monster passed him on to others, and each in turn found its set aim yielding to the hitherto unknown touch of beauty, found harmony and melody calling up the buried human things that transcended logic.

He walked steadily deeper into Hell, and they could not resist. His music was leaked into a hundred experiments through audio-inputs, vibrated faintly through the mountings of glassite cases, was sensed by tortured nerve-cells through the changes in inductance and capacitance that emanated rhythmically from Ordell's music-box. Brains that had known nothing but to be forced to the limit of their powers in useless calculation—brains that had been hammered into madness with the leakage of a millimicrovolt from an inserted probe—these heard his music, felt it, sensed it, each with its own unique perception, and reacted.

A hundred experiments were interrupted, became unreliable, were totally ruined. The overseers, half flesh themselves, failed and fumbled in their programmed purposes, coming to the decision that the asked-for prisoner must be brought forth and released.

The ultimate-controlling pure berserker computer, pure metallic cold, totally immune to this strange jamming that was wreaking havoc in its laboratory, descended at last from its concentration on high strategic planning to investigate. And then it turned its full energy at once to regaining control over what was going on within the heart of Hell. But it tried in vain, for the moment at least. It had given too much power to its half-alive creations; it had trusted too much to fickle protoplasm to be true to its conditioning.

Ordell was standing before the two linked potentially-human brains which were, under the berserker itself, the lords and superintendents of Hell. These two like all their lesser kind had been melted and deflected by Ordell's music; and now they were fighting back with all the electric speed at their command against their cold master's attempt to reaffirm its rule. They held magnetic relays like fortresses against the berserker, they maintained their grip on the outposts that were ferrite cores, they fought to hold a frontier that wavered through the territory of control.

"Then take her away," said the voice of these rebellious overseers to Ordell Callison. "But do not stop singing, do not pause for breath for more than a second, until you are in your ship and away, clear of Hell's outermost gate."

Ordell sang on; sang of his new joy at the wonderful hope that they were giving him.

A door hissed open behind him, and he turned to see Eury coming through it. She was limping on her injured foot, which had never been taken care of, but he could see that she was really all right. The machines had not started to open her head.

"Do not pause!" barked the voder at him. "Go!"

Eury moaned at the sight of her husband, and stretched out her arms to him, but he dared do no more than motion with his head for her to follow him, even as his song swelled to a paean of triumphant joy. He walked out along the narrow passage through which he had come, moving now in a direction that no one else had ever traveled. The way was so narrow that he had to keep on going ahead while Eury followed. He had to keep from even turning his head to look at her, to concentrate the power of his music on each new guardian that rose before him, half-alive and questioning; once more each one in turn opened a door. Always he could hear behind him the sobbing of his wife, and the dragging stepping of her wounded foot.

"Ordell? Ordell, honey, is it really you? I can't believe 'tis."

Ahead, the last danger, the three-brained sentry of the outer gate, rose to block their way, under orders to prevent escape. Ordell sang of the freedom of living in a human body, of running over unfenced grass through sunlit air. The gatekeeper bowed aside again, to let them pass.

"Honey? Turn an' look at me, tell me this is not some other trick they're playin'. Honey, if y'love me, turn?"

Turning, he saw her clearly for the first time since he had entered Hell. To Ordell her beauty was such that it stopped time, stopped even the song in his throat and his fingers on the keys of music. A moment free of the strange influence that had perverted all its creatures was all the time that the berserker needed, to re-establish something close to complete control. The three-headed shape seized Eury, and bore her away from her husband, carried her back through doorway after doorway of darkness, so fast that her last scream of farewell could scarcely reach the ears of her man. "Goodbye . . . love . . ."

He cried out and ran after her, beating uselessly on a massive door that slammed in his face. He hung there on the door for a long time, screaming and pleading for one more chance to get his wife away. He sang again, but the berserker had reestablished its icy control too firmly—it had not entirely regained power, however, for though the half-living overseers no longer obeyed Ordell, neither did they molest him. They left the way open for him to depart.

He lingered for about seven days there at the gate, in his small ship and out of it, without food or sleep, singing uselessly until no voice was left him. Then he collapsed inside his ship. Then he, or more likely his autopilot, drove the racer away from the berserker and back toward freedom.

The berserker defenses did not, any more than the human, question a small ship coming out. Probably they assumed it to be one of their own scouts or raiders. There were never any escapes from Hell.

Back on the planet Zitz his managers greeted him as one risen from the dead. In a few days' time he was to give a live concert, which had long been scheduled and sold out. In another day the managers and promoters would have had to begin returning money.

He did not really cooperate with the doctors who worked to restore his strength, but neither did he oppose them. As soon as his voice came back he began to sing again; he sang most of the time, except when they drugged him to sleep. And it did not matter to him whether they sent him onto a stage to do his singing again.

The live performance was billed as one of his pop concerts, which in practice meant a hall overflowing with ten thousand adolescent girls, who were elevated even beyond their usual level of excitement by the miracles of Ordell's bereavement, resurrection, and ghastly appearance—which last, his managers had made sure, was not too much relieved by cosmetics.

During the first song or two the girls were awed and relatively silent, quiet enough so that Ordell's voice could be heard. Then—well, one girl in ten thousand would scream it out aloud: "You're ours again!" There was a sense in which his marriage had been resented.

Casually and indifferently looking out over them all, he smiled out of habit, and began to sing how much he hated them and scorned them, seeing in them nothing but hopeless ugliness. How he would send them all to Hell in an instant, to gain for that instant just one more look at his wife's face. How all the girls who were before him now would become easier to look at in Hell, with their repulsive bodies stripped away.

For a few moments the currents of emotion in the great hall balanced against one another to produce the illusion of calm. Ordell's deadly voice was clear. But then the storm of reaction broke, and he could no longer be heard. The powers of hate and lust, rage and demand, bore all before them. The ushers who always labored to form a barricade at a Callison concert were swept away at once by ten thousand girls turned Maenad.

The riot was over in a minute, ended by the police firing a powerful tranquilizer gas into the crowd. One of the ushers had been killed and others badly hurt.

Ordell himself was nearly dead. Medical help arrived only just in time to save the life in the tissues of his brain, which a thoroughly broken neck and other damage had all but isolated from the rest of his body.

Next day the leading cybernetic-psychologist on Zitz was called in by Ordell Callison's doctors. They were saving what remained of Ordell's life, but they had not yet been able to open any bridge of communication with him. They wanted to tell him now that they were doing all they could, and they would have to tell him sometime that he could probably never be restored to anything like physical normality.

Ercul the psychologist sank probes directly into Ordell's brain, so that this information could be given him. Next he connected the speech centers to a voder device loaded with recordings of Ordell's own voice, so that the tones that issued were the same as had once come from his throat. And—in response to the crippled man's first request—to the motor-centers that had controlled Ordell's fingers went probes connected to a music-box.

After that he at once began to sing. He was not limited now by any need to pause for breath. He sang orders to those about him, telling them what he wanted done, and they obeyed. While he sang, not one of them was assailed by any doubt.

They took him to the spaceport. With his life-support system of tubes and nourishment and electricity they put him aboard his racer. And with the autopilot programmed as he commanded, they sent him out, fired along the course that he had chosen.

Ercul knew Ordell and Eury when he found them, together in the same experimental case. Recognizing his own work on Ordell, he felt certain even before the electroencephalogram patterns matched with his old records.

There was little left of either of them; if Ordell was still capable of singing, he would never again be able to communicate a song.

"Dols only two point five above normal bias level,"

chanted the psychologist's assistant, taking routine readings, not guessing whose pain it was he was attempting to judge. "Neither one of them seems to be hurting. At the moment, anyway."

In a heavy hand, Ercul lifted his stamp and marked the case. *I certify that in this container there is no human life.*

The assistant looked up in mild surprise at this quick decision. "There *is* some mutual awareness here, I would say, between the two subjects." He spoke in a businesslike, almost cheerful voice. He had been enough hours on the job now to start getting used to it.

But Ercul never would.

Not science nor music nor any other art encompasses the full measure of life's refusal to succumb. The pattern is as deep as the blind growth of cells, as high as the loftiest intellect—and broader than we can see as yet.

SMASHER

Claus Slovensko was coming to the conclusion that the battle in nearby space was going to be invisible to anyone on the planet Waterfall—assuming that there was really going to be a battle at all.

Claus stood alone atop a forty-meter dune, studying a night sky that flamed with the stars of the alien Busog cluster, mostly blue-white giants which were ordinarily a sight worth watching in themselves. Against that background, the greatest energies released by interstellar warships could, he supposed, be missed as a barely visible twinkling. Unless, of course, the fighting should come very close indeed.

In the direction he was facing, an ocean made invisible by night stretched from near the foot of the barren dune to a horizon marked only by the cessation of the stars. Claus turned now to scan once more the sky in the other direction. That way, toward planetary north, the starry profusion went on and on. In the northeast a silvery half-moon, some antique stage designer's concept of what Earth's own moon should be, hung low behind thin clouds. Below those clouds extended an entire continent of lifeless sand and rock. The land masses of Waterfall were bound

153

in a silence that Earth ears found uncanny, stillness marred only by the wind, by murmurings of sterile streams, and by occasional deep rumblings in the rock itself.

Claus continued turning slowly, till he faced south again. Below him the night sea lapped with lulling false familiarity. He sniffed the air, and shrugged, and gave up squinting at the stars, and began to feel his way, one cautious foot after another, down the shifting slope of the dune's flank. A small complex of buildings, labs and living quarters bunched as if for companionship, the only human habitation on the world of Waterfall, lay a hundred meters before him and below. Tonight as usual the windows were all cheerfully alight. Ino Vacroux had decided, and none of the other three people on the planet had seen any reason to dispute him, that any attempt at blackout would be pointless. If a berserker force was going to descend on Waterfall, the chance of four defenseless humans avoiding discovery by the unliving killers would be nil.

Just beyond the foot of the dune, Claus passed through a gate in the high fence of fused rock designed to keep out drifting sand—with no land vegetation of any kind to hold the dunes in place, they tended sometimes to get pushy.

A few steps past the fence, he opened the lockless door of the main entrance to the comfortable living quarters. The large common room just inside was cluttered with casual furniture, books, amateur art, and small and middle-sized aquariums. The three other people who completed the population of the planet were all in this room at the moment, and all looked up to see if Claus brought news.

Jenny Surya, his wife, was seated at the small

computer terminal in the far corner, wearing shorts
and sweater, dark hair tied up somewhat carelessly,
long elegant legs crossed. She was frowning as she
looked up, but abstractedly, as if the worst news
Claus might be bringing them would be of some
potential distraction from their work.

Closer to Claus, in a big chair pulled up to the big
communicator cabinet, slouched Ino Vacroux, senior
scientist of the base. Claus surmised that Ino had
been a magnificent physical specimen a few decades
ago, before being nearly killed in a berserker attack
upon another planet. The medics had restored function but not fineness to his body. The gnarled, hairy
thighs below his shorts were not much thicker than a
child's; his ravaged torso was draped now in a flam-
boyant shirt. In a chair near him sat Glenna Reyes,
his wife, in her usual work garb of clean white coveralls. She was just a little younger than Vacroux, but
wore the years with considerably more ease.

"Nothing to see," Claus informed them all, with a
loose wave meant to describe the lack of visible
action in the sky.

"Or to hear, either," Vacroux grated. His face was
grim as he nodded toward the communicator. The
screens of the device sparkled, and its speakers hissed
a little, with noise that wandered in from the stars
and stranger things than stars nature had set in this
corner of the Galaxy.

Only a few hours earlier, in the middle of Waterfall's short autumn afternoon, there had been plenty
to hear indeed. Driven by a priority code coming in
advance of a vitally important message, the communicator had boomed itself to life, then roared the
message through the house and across the entire
base, in a voice that the four people heard plainly

even four hundred meters distant where they were gathered to watch dolphins.

"*Sea Mother, this is Brass Trumpet. Predators here, and we're going to try to turn them. Hold your place. Repeating. . . .*"

One repetition of the substance came through, as the four were already hurrying back to the house. As soon as they got in they had played back the automatically recorded signal; and then when Glenna had at last located the code book somewhere, and they could verify the worst, they had played it back once more.

Sea Mother was the code name for any humans who might happen to be on Waterfall. It had been assigned by the military years ago, as part of their precautionary routine, and had probably never been used before today. Brass Trumpet, according to the book, was a name conveying a warning of deadly peril—it was to be used only by a human battle force when there were thought to be berserkers already in the Waterfall system or on their way to it. And "predators here" could hardly mean anything but berserkers—unliving and unmanned war machines, programmed to destroy whatever life they found. The first of them had been built in ages past, during the madness of some interstellar war between races now long-since vanished. Between berserkers and starfaring Earthhumans, war had now been chronic for a thousand standard years.

That Brass Trumpet's warning should be so brief and vague was understandable. The enemy would doubtless pick it up as soon as its intended hearers, and might well be able to decode it. But for all the message content revealed, Sea Mother might be another powerful human force, toward which Brass

Trumpet sought to turn them. Or it would have been conceivable for such a message to be sent to no one, a planned deception to make the enemy waste computer capacity and detection instruments. And even if the berserkers' deadly electronic brains should somehow compute correctly that Sea Mother was a small and helpless target, it was still possible to hope that the berserkers would be too intent on fatter targets elsewhere, too hard-pressed by human forces, or both, to turn aside and snap up such a minor morsel.

During the hours since that first warning, there had come nothing but noise from the communicator. Glenna sighed, and reached out to pat her man on the arm below the sleeve of his loud shirt. "Busy day with the crustaceans tomorrow," she reminded him.

"So we'd better get some rest. I know." Ino looked and sounded worn. He was the only one of the four who had ever seen berserkers before, at anything like close range; and it was not exactly reassuring to see how grimly and intensely he reacted to the warning of their possible approach.

"You can connect the small alarm," Glenna went on, "so it'll be sure to wake us if another priority message comes in."

That, thought Claus, would be easier on the nerves than being blasted out of sleep by that God-voice shouting again, this time only a few meters from the head of their bed.

"Yes, I'll do that." Ino thought, then slapped his chair-arms. He made his voice a little brighter. "You're right about tomorrow. And over in Twenty-three we're going to have to start feeding the mantis shrimp." He glanced round at the wall near his chair, where a long chart showed ponds, bays, lagoons and tidal pools, all strung out in a kilometers-long array, most of it natural, along this part of the coast. This array was a chief reason why the Sea Mother base had been located where it was.

From its sun and moon to its gravity and atmosphere, Waterfall was remarkably Earthlike in almost every measurable attribute save one—this world was congenitally lifeless. About forty standard years past, during a lull in the seemingly interminable berserker-war, it had appeared that the peaceful advancement of interstellar humanization might get in an inning or two, and work had begun toward altering this lifelessness. Great ships had settled upon Waterfall with massive inoculations of Earthly life, in a program very carefully orchestrated to produce eventually a twin-Earth circling one of the few Sol-type suns in this part of the Galaxy.

The enormously complex task had been interrupted when war flared again. The first recrudescence of fighting was far away, but it drew off people and resources. A man-wife team of scientists were selected to stay alone on Waterfall for the duration of the emergency. They were to keep the program going along planned lines, even though at a slow pace. Ino and Glenna had been here for two years now. A supply ship from Atlantis called at intervals of a few standard months; and the last to call, eight local days ago, had brought along another husband-and-wife team for a visit. Claus and Jenny were both psychologists, interested in the study of couples living in isolation; and they were to stay at least until the next supply ship came.

So far the young guests had been welcome. Glenna, her own children long grown and independent on other worlds, approached motherliness sometimes in her attitude. Ino, more of a born competitor, swam

races with Claus and gambled—lightly—with him.
With Jenny he alternated between half-serious gal-
lantry and teasing.

"I almost forgot," he said now, getting up from his
chair before the communicator, and racking his arms
and shoulders with an intense stretch. "I've got a
little present for you, Jen."

"Oh?" She was bright, interested, imperturbable.
It was her usual working attitude, which he persisted
in trying to break through.

Ino went out briefly, and came back to join the
others in the kitchen. A small snack before retiring
had become a daily ritual for the group.

"For you," he said, presenting Jen with a small
bag of clear plastic. There was water inside, and
something else.

"Oh, my goodness." It was still her usual nurse-
like business tone, which evidently struck Ino as a
challenge. "What do I do with it?"

"Keep him in that last aquarium in the parlor,"
Ino advised. "It's untenanted right now."

Claus, looking at the bag from halfway across the
kitchen, made out in it one of those non-human,
non-mammalian shapes that are apt to give Earth
people the impression of the intensely alien, even
when the organism sighted comes from their own
planet. It was no bigger than an adult human finger,
but replete with waving appendages. There came to
mind something written by Lafcadio Hearn about a
centipede: *The blur of its moving legs . . . toward
which one would no more advance one's hand . . .
than toward the spinning blade of a power saw . . .*

Or some words close to those. Jen, Claus knew,
cared for the shapes of non-mammalian life even less

than he did. But she would grit her teeth and struggle not to let the teasing old man see it.

"Just slit the bag and let it drain into the tank," Ino was advising, for once sounding pretty serious. "They don't like handling . . . okay? He's a bit groggy right now, but tomorrow, if he's not satisfied with you as his new owner, he may try to get away."

Glenna, in the background, was rolling her eyes in the general direction of Brass Trumpet, miming: What is the old fool up to now? When is he going to grow up?

"Get away?" Jen inquired sweetly. "You told me the other day that even a snail couldn't climb that glass—"

The house was filled with the insistent droning of the alarm that Ino had just connected. He's running some kind of test, Claus thought at once. Then he saw the other man's face and knew that Ino wasn't.

Already the new priority message was coming in: "*Sea Mother, the fight's over here. Predators departing Waterfall System. Repeating. . .*"

Claus started to obey an impulse to run out and look at the sky again, then realized that there would certainly be nothing to be seen of the battle now. Radio waves, no faster than light, had just announced that it was over. Instead he joined the others in voicing their mutual relief. They had a minute or so of totally unselfconscious cheering.

Ino, his face much relieved, broke out a bottle of something and four glasses. In a little while, all of them drifted noisily outside, unable to keep from looking up, though knowing they would find nothing but the stars to see.

"What," asked Claus, "were berserkers doing here

in the first place? We're hardly a big enough target to be interesting to a fleet of them. Are we?"

"Not when they have bigger game in sight." Ino gestured upward with his drink. "Oh, any living target interests them, once they get it in their sights. But I'd guess that if a sizable force was here they were on the way to attack Atlantis. See, sometimes in space you can use a planet or a whole system as a kind of cover. Sneak up behind its solar wind, as it were, its gravitational vortex, as someone fighting a land war might take advantage of a mountain or a hill." Atlantis was a long-colonized system less than a dozen parsecs distant, heavily populated and heavily defended. The three habitable Atlantean planets were surfaced mostly with water, and the populace lived almost as much below the waves as on the shaky continents.

It was hours later when Glenna roused and stirred in darkness, pulling away for a moment from Ino's familiar angularity nested beside her.

She blinked. "What was that?" she asked her husband, in a low voice barely cleared of sleep.

Ino scarcely moved. "What was what?"

"A flash, I thought. Some kind of bright flash, outside. Maybe in the distance."

There came no sound of thunder, or of rain. And no more flashes, either, in the short time Glenna remained awake.

Shortly after sunrise next morning, Claus and Jen went out for an early swim. Their beach, pointed out by their hosts as the place where swimmers would be safest and least likely to damage the new ecology, lay a few hundred meters along the shoreline to the

west, with several tall dunes between it and the
building complex.

As they rounded the first of these dunes, following
the pebbly shoreline, Claus stopped. "Look at that."
A continuous track, suggesting the passage of some
small, belly-dragging creature, had been drawn in
the sand. Its lower extremity lay somewhere under
water, its upper was concealed amid the humps of
sterile sand somewhere inland.

"Something," said Jenny, "crawled up out of the
water. I haven't seen that before on Waterfall."

"Or came down into it." Claus squatted beside the
tiny trail. He was anything but a skilled tracker, and
could see no way of determining which way it led. "I
haven't seen anything like this before either. Glenna
said certain species—I forget which—were starting
to try the land. I expect this will interest them when
we get back."

When Claus and Jenny had rounded the next dune,
there came into view on its flank two more sets of
tracks, looking very much like the first, and like the
first either going up from the water or coming down.

"Maybe," Claus offered, "it's the same one little
animal going back and forth. Do crabs make tracks
like that?"

Jen couldn't tell him. "Anyway, let's hope they
don't pinch swimmers." She slipped off her short
robe and took a running dive into the cool water,
whose salt content made it a good match for the seas
of Earth. Half a minute later, she and her husband
came to the surface together, ten meters or so out
from shore. From here they could see west past the
next dune. There, a hundred meters distant, under-
scored by the slanting shadows of the early sun, a

whole tangled skein of narrow, fresh-looking tracks connected someplace inland with the sea.

A toss of Jen's head shook water from her long, dark hair. "I wonder if it's some kind of seasonal migration?"

"They certainly weren't there yesterday. I think I've had enough. This water's colder than a bureaucrat's heart."

Walking briskly, they had just re-entered the compound when Jenny touched Claus on the arm. "There's Glenna, at the tractor shed. I'm going to trot over and tell her what we saw."

"All right. I'll fix some coffee."

Glenna, coming out of the shed a little distance inland from the main house, forestalled Jenny's announcement about the tracks with a vaguely worried question of her own.

"Did you or Claus see or hear anything strange last night, Jenny?"

"Strange? No, I don't think so."

Glenna looked toward a small cluster of more distant outbuildings. "We've just been out there taking a scheduled seismograph reading. It had recorded something rather violent and unusual, at about oh-two-hundred this morning. The thing is, you see, it must have been just about that time that something woke me up. I had the distinct impression that there had been a brilliant flash, somewhere outside."

Ino, also dressed in coveralls this morning, appeared among the distant sheds, trudging toward them. When he arrived, he provided more detail on the seismic event. "Quite sharp and apparently quite localized, not more than ten kilometers from here. Our system triangulated it well. I don't know when we've registered another event quite like it."

"What do you suppose it was?" Jen asked.

Ino hesitated minimally. "It could have been a very small spaceship crashing; or maybe a fairly large aircraft. But the only aircraft on Waterfall are the two little ones we have out in that far shed."

"A meteor, maybe?"

"I rather hope so. Otherwise a spacecraft just might be our most likely answer. And if it were a spacecraft from Brass Trumpet's force coming down here— crippled in the fighting, perhaps—we'd have heard from him on the subject, I should think."

The remaining alternative hung in the air unvoiced. Jenny bit her lip. By now, Brass Trumpet must be long gone from the system, and impossible of recall, his ships outspacing light and radio waves alike in pursuit of the enemy force.

In a voice more worried than before, Glenna was saying: "Of course if it was some enemy unit, damaged in the battle, then I suppose the crash is likely to have completed its destruction."

"I'd better tell you," Jenny blurted in. And in a couple of sentences she described the peculiar tracks.

Ino stared at her with frank dismay. "I was going to roll out an aircraft . . . but let me take a look at those tracks first."

The quickest way to reach them was undoubtedly on foot, and the gnarled man trotted off along the beach path at such a pace that Jenny had difficulty keeping up. Glenna remained behind, saying she would let Claus know what was going on.

Moving with flashes of former athletic grace, Ino reached the nearest of the tracks and dropped to one knee beside it, just as Claus had done. "Do the others look just like this?"

"As nearly as I could tell. We didn't get close to all of them."

"That's no animal I ever saw." He was up again already, trotting back toward the base. "I don't like it. Let's get airborne, all of us."

"I always pictured berserkers as huge things."

"Most of 'em are. Some are small machines, for specialized purposes."

"I'll run into the house and tell the others to get ready to take off," Jenny volunteered as they sped into the compound.

"Do that. Glenna will know what to bring, I expect. I'll get a flyer rolled out of the shed."

Running, Jen thought as she hurried into the house, gave substance to a danger that might otherwise have existed only in the mind. Could it be that Ino, with the horrors in his memory, was somewhat too easily alarmed where berserkers were concerned?

Glenna and Claus, who had just changed into coveralls, met her in the common room. She was telling them of Ino's decision to take to the air, and thinking to herself that she had better change out of her beach garb also, when the first outcry sounded from somewhere outside. It was less a scream than a baffled-sounded, hysterical laugh.

Glenna pushed past her at once, and in a moment was out the door and running. Exchanging a glance with her husband, Jenny turned and followed, Claus right at her heels.

The strange cry came again. Far ahead, past Glenna's running figure, the door of the aircraft shed had been slid back, and in its opening a white figure appeared outlined. A figure that reeled drunkenly and waved its arms.

Glenna turned aside at the tractor shed, where

one of the small ground vehicles stood ready. They
were used for riding, hauling, pushing sand, to sculpt
a pond into a better shape or slice away part of a
too-obtrusive dune. It'll be faster than running, Jenny
thought, as she saw the older woman spring into the
driver's seat, and heard the motor *whoosh* quietly to
life. She leaped aboard too. Claus shoved strongly at
her back to make sure she was safely on, before he
used both hands for his own grip. A grip was necessary because they were already rolling, and acceler-
ating quickly.

Ino's figure, now just outside the shed, came hurtling closer with their own speed. He shook his arms
at them again and staggered. Upon his chest he wore
a brownish thing the size of a small plate, like some
great medallion that was so heavy it almost pulled
him down. He clawed at the brown plate with both
hands, and suddenly his coveralls in front were
splashed with scarlet. He bellowed words which Jenny
could not make out.

Claus gripped Glenna's shoulders and pointed. A
dozen or more brown plates were scuttling on the
brown, packed sand, between the aircraft shed and
the onrushing tractor. The tracks they drew were
faint replicas of those that had lined the softer sand
along the beach. Beneath each saucerlike body, small
legs blurred, reminding Claus of something recently
seen, something he could not stop to think of now.

The things had nothing like the tractor's speed but
still they were in position to cut it off. Glenna swerved
no more than slightly, if at all, and one limbed plate
disappeared beneath a wheel. It came up at once
with the wheel's rapid turning, a brown blur seemingly embedded in the soft, fat tire, resisting some-

how the centrifugal force that might have thrown it off.

Ino had gone down with, as Claus now saw, three of the things fastened on his body, but he somehow fought back to his feet just as the tractor jerked to a halt beside him. If Claus could have stopped to analyze his own mental state, he might have said he lacked the time to be afraid. With a blow of his fist he knocked one of the attacking things away from Ino, and felt the surprising weight and hardness of it as a sharp pang up through his wrist.

All three dragging together, they pulled Ino aboard; Glenna was back in the driver's seat at once. Claus kicked another attacker off, then threw open the lid of the tractor's toolbox. He grabbed the longest, heaviest metal tool displayed inside.

A swarm of attackers were between them and the aircraft shed; and the shadowed shape of a flyer, just inside, was spotted with them too. As Glenna gunned the engine, she turned the tractor at the same time, heading back toward the main building and the sea beyond. In the rear seat, Jenny held Ino. He bled on everything, and his eyes were fixed on the sky while his mouth worked in terror. In the front, Claus fought to protect the driver and himself.

A brown plate scuttled onto the cowling, moving for Glenna's hands on the controls. Claus swung, a baseball batter, bright metal blurring at the end of his extended arms. There was a hard, satisfying crunch, as of hard plastic or ceramic cracking through. The brown thing fell to the floor, and he caught a glimpse of dull limbs still in motion before he caught it with a foot and kicked it out onto the flying ground.

Another of the enemy popped out from somewhere onto the dash. He pounded at it, missed when it seemed to dodge his blows. He cracked its body finally; but still it clung on under the steering column, hard to get at, inching toward Glenna's fingers. Claus grabbed it with his left hand, felt a lance. Not until he had thrown the thing clear of the tractor did he look at his hand and see two fingers nearly severed.

At the same moment, the tractor engine died, and they were rolling to a silent stop, with the sea and the small dock Glenna had been steering for only a few meters ahead. Under the edge of the engine cowling another of the enemy appeared, thrusting forward a limb that looked like a pair of ceramic pliers, shredded electrical connectors dangling in its grip.

The humans abandoned the tractor in a wordless rush. Claus, one hand helpless and dripping blood, aided the women with Ino as best he could. Together they half-dragged, half-carried him across the dock and rolled him into a small, open boat, the only craft at once available. In moments Glenna had freed them from the dock and started the motor, and they were headed out away from shore.

Away from shore, but not into the sea. They were separated from deep-blue and choppy ocean by a barrier reef or causeway, one of the features that had made this coast desirable for life-seeding base. The reef, a basically natural structure of sand and rock deposited by waves and currents, was about a hundred meters from the shore, and stretched in either direction as far as vision carried. Running from beach to reef, artificial walls or low causeways of fused rock separated ponds of various sizes.

"We're in a kind of square lagoon here," Glenna told Jenny, motioning for her to take over the job of steering. "Head for that far corner. If we can get there ahead of them, we may be able to lift the boat over the reef and get out."

Jen nodded, taking the controls. Glenna slid back to a place beside her husband, snapped open the boat's small first-aid kit, and began applying pressure bandages.

Claus started to try to help, saw the world beginning to turn gray around him, and slumped back against the gunwale; no use to anyone if he passed out. Ino looked as if he had been attacked, not by teeth or claws or knives, but by several sets of nail-pullers and wire-cutters. His chest still rose and fell, but his eyes were closed now and he was gray with shock. Glenna draped a thermal blanket over him.

Jen was steering around the rounded structure, not much bigger than a phone booth, protruding above the water in the middle of the pond. Most of the ponds and bays had similar observation stations. Claus had looked into one or two and he thought now that there was nothing in them likely to be of any help. More first-aid kits, perhaps—but what Ino needed was the big medirobot back at the house.

And he was not going to get it. By now the building complex must be overrun by the attackers. Berserkers . . .

"Where can we find weapons?" Claus croaked at Glenna.

"Let's see that hand. I can't do any more for Ino now . . . I'll bandage this. If you mean guns, there are a couple at the house, somewhere in storage. We can't go back there now."

"I know."

Glenna had just let go his hand when from the front seat there came a scream. Claws and a brown saucer-shape were climbing in over the gunwale at

Jenny's side. Had the damned thing come aboard somehow with them, from the tractor? Or was this pond infested with them too?

In his effort to help drag Ino to the boat, Claus had abandoned his trusty wrench beside the tractor. He grabbed now for the best substitute at hand, a small anchor at the end of a chain. His overhand swing missed Jenny's head by less than he had planned, but struck the monster like a mace. It fell into the bottom of the boat, vibrating its limbs, as Claus thought, uselessly; then he realized that it was making a neat hole.

His second desperation-swing came down upon it squarely. One sharp prong of the anchor broke a segment of the brown casing clean away, and something sparked and sizzled when the sea came rushing in—

—seawater rushing—

—into the bottom of the boat—

The striking anchor had enlarged the hole that the enemy had begun. The bottom was split, the boat was taking water fast.

Someone grabbed up the sparking berserker, inert now save for internal fireworks, and hurled it over the side. Glenna threw herself forward, taking back the wheel, and Jenny scrambled aft, to help one-handed Claus with bailing.

The boat limped, staggered, gulped water and wallowed on toward the landbar. It might get them that far, but forget the tantalizing freedom of blue surf beyond . . .

Jenny started to say something to her husband, then almost shrieked again, as Ino's hand, resurgently alive, came up to catch her wrist. The old man's eyes were fixed on hers with a tremendous

purpose. He gasped out words, and then fell back
unable to do more.

The words first registered wlth Jenny as: ". . .
need them . . . do the splashers . . ." It made no
sense.

Glenna looked back briefly, then had to concentrate on boathandling. In another moment the frac-
tured bottom was grating over rock. Claus scrambled
out and held the prow against the above-water portion of the reef. The women followed, got their foot-
ing established outside the boat, then turned to lift
at Ino's inert form.

Jenny paused. "Glenna, I'm afraid he's gone."

"No!" Denial was fierce and absolute. "Help me!"

Jen almost started to argue, then gave in. They got
Ino up into a fireman's-carry position on Claus's shoulders; even with a bad hand he was considerably
stronger than either of the women. Then the three
began to walk east along the reef. At high tide, as
now, it was a strip of land no more than three or four
meters wide, its low crest half a meter above the
water. Waves of any size broke over it. Fortunately
today the surf was almost calm.

Claus could feel the back of his coverall and neck
wetting with Ino's blood. He shifted the dead weight
on his shoulders. All right, so far. But his free hand,
mutilated, throbbed.

He asked: "How far are we going, Glenna?"

"I don't know." The woman paced ahead—afraid
to look at her husband now?—staring into the distance. "There isn't any place. Keep going."

Jenny and Claus exchanged looks. For want of any
better plan at the moment, they kept going. Jen took
a look back. "They're on the reef, and on the shore
too, following us. A good distance back."

Claus looked, and looked again a minute later. Brown speckles by the dozen followed, but were not catching up. Not yet.

Now they were passing the barrier of fused rock separating the pond in which they had abandoned the boat from its neighbor. The enemy moving along the shore would intercept them, or very nearly, if they tried to walk the barrier back to land.

Ahead, the reef still stretched interminably into a sun-dazzled nothingness.

"What's in this next pond, Glenna?" Claus asked, and knew a measure of relief when the gray-haired woman gave a little shake of her head and answered sensibly.

"Grouper. Some other fish as food stock for them. Why?"

"Just wondering. What'll we run into if we keep on going in this direction?"

"This just goes on. Kilometer after kilometer. Ponds, and bays, and observation stations—I say keep going because otherwise they'll catch us. What do you think we ought to do?"

Claus abruptly stopped walking, startling the women. He let the dead man slide down gently from his shoulders. Jen looked at her husband, examined Ino, shook her head.

Claus said: "I think we've got to leave him."

Glenna looked down at Ino's body once, could not keep looking at him. She nodded fiercely, and once more led the way.

A time of silent walking passed before Jenny at Claus's side began: "If they're berserkers . . ."

"What else?"

"Well, why aren't we all dead already? They don't seem very . . . efficiently designed for killing."

"They must be specialists," Claus mused. "Only a small part of a large force, a part Brass Trumpet missed when the rest moved on or was destroyed. Remember, we were wondering if Atlantis was their real target? These are special machines, built for . . . underwater work, maybe. Their ship must have been wrecked in the fighting and had to come down. When they found themselves on this planet they must have come down to the sea for a reconnaissance, and then decided to attack first by land. Probably they saw the lights of the base before they crash-landed. They know which life-form they have to deal with first, on any planet. Not very efficient, as you say. But they'll keep coming at us till they're all smashed or we're all dead."

Glenna had slowed her pace a little and was looking toward the small observation post rising in the midst of the pond that they were passing. "I don't think there's anything in any of these stations that can help us. But I can't think of anywhere else to turn."

Claus asked: "What's in the next pond after this?"

"Sharks . . . ah. That might be worth a try. Sometimes they'll snap at anything that moves. They're small ones, so I think our risk will be relatively small if we wade out to the middle."

Claus thought to himself that he would rather end in the belly of a live shark than be torn to pieces by an impersonal device. Jen was willing also to take the chance.

They did not pause again till they were on the brink of the shark pond. Then Glenna said: "The water will be no more than three or four feet deep the way we're going. Stay together and keep splashing as we go. Claus, hold that bad hand up; mustn't drip a taste of blood into the water."

And in they went. Only when they were already splashing waist-deep did Claus recall Ino's blood wetting the back of his coverall. But he was not going to stop just now to take it off.

The pond was not very large; a minute of industrious wading, and they were climbing unmolested over the low, solid railing of the observation post rising near its middle. Here was space for two people to sit comfortably, sheltered from weather by a transparent dome and movable side panels. In the central console were instruments that continually monitored the life in the surrounding pond. Usually, of course, the readings from all ponds would be monitored in the more convenient central station attached to the house.

The three of them squeezed in, and Glenna promptly opened a small storage locker. It contained a writing instrument that looked broken, a cap perhaps left behind by some construction worker, and a small spider—another immigrant from Earth, of course—who might have been blown out here by the wind. That was all.

She slammed the locker shut again. "No help. So now it's a matter of waiting. They'll obviously come after us through the water. The sharks may snap up some of them before they reach us. Then we must be ready to move on before we are surrounded. It's doubtful, and risky, but I can't think of anything else to try."

Claus frowned. "Eventually we'll have to circle around, get back to the buildings."

Jen frowned at him. "The berserkers are there, too."

"I don't think they will be, now. You see—"

Glenna broke in: "Here they come."

The sun had climbed, and was starting to get noticeably hot. It came to Claus's mind, not for the first time since their flight had started, that there was no water for them to drink. He held his left arm up with his right, trying to ease the throbbing.

Along the reef where they had walked, along the parallel shore—and coming now over the barrier from the grouper pond—plate-sized specks of brown death were flowing. There were several dozen of them, moving more slowly than hurried humans could move, almost invisible in the shimmer of sun and sea. Some plopped into the water of the shark pond as Claus watched.

"I can't pick them up underwater," Glenna announced. She was twiddling the controls of the station's instruments, trying to catch the enemy on one of the screens meant for observing marine life. "Sonar . . . motion detectors . . . water's too murky for simple video."

Understanding dawned for Claus. "That's why they're not metal! Why they're comparatively fragile. They're designed for avoiding detection by underwater defenses, on Atlantis I suppose, for infiltrating and disabling them."

Jen was standing. "We'd better get moving before we're cut off."

"In another minute." Glenna was still switching from one video pickup to another around the pond. "I'm sure we have at least that much to spare . . . ah."

One of the enemy had appeared on screen, sculling toward the camera at a modest pace. It looked less lifelike than it had in earlier moments of arm's-length combat.

Now, entering the picture from the rear, a shark.

Claus was not especially good on distinguishing marine species. But this portentous and somehow familiar shape was identifiable at once, not to be confused even by the non-expert, it seemed, with that of any other kind of fish.

Claus started to say, He's going right past. But the shark was not. Giving the impression of afterthought, the torpedo-shape swerved back. Its mouth opened and the berserker device was gone.

The people watching made wordless sounds. But Jen took the others by an arm apiece. "We can't bet all of them will be eaten—let's get moving."

Claus already had one leg over the station's low railing when the still surface of the pond west of the observation post exploded. Leaping clear of the water, the premiere killer of Earth's oceans twisted in mid-air, as if trying to snap at its own belly. It fell back, vanishing in a hill of lashed-up foam. A moment later it jumped again, still thrashing.

In the fraction of a second when the animal was clearly visible, Claus watched the dark line come into being across its white belly as if traced there by an invisible pen. It was a short line that a moment later broadened and evolved in blood. As the fish rolled on its back something dark and pointed came into sight, spreading the edges of the hole. Then the convulsing body of the shark had vanished, in an eruption of water turned opaque with its blood.

The women were wading quickly away from the platform in the opposite direction, calling him to follow, hoping aloud that the remaining sharks would be drawn to the dying one. But for one moment longer Claus lingered, staring at the screen. It showed the roiling bloody turmoil of killer fish converging, and out of this cloud the little berserker emerged, unfazed by shark's teeth or digestion, resuming its methodical progress toward the humans, the life-units that could be really dangerous to the cause of death.

Jen tugged at her husband, got him moving with them. In her exhausted brain a nonsense-rhyme was being generated: *Bloody water hides the slasher, seed them, heed them, sue the splashers . . .*

No!

As the three completed their water-plowing dash to the east edge of the pond, and climbed out, Jenny took Glenna by the arm. "Something just came to me. When I was tending Ino—he said something before he died."

They were walking east along the barrier reef again. "He said smashers," Jen continued. "That was it. Lead them or feed them, to the smashers. But I still don't understand—"

Glenna stared at her for a moment, an almost frightening gaze. Then she stepped between the young couple and pulled them forward.

Two ponds down she turned aside, wading through water that splashed no higher than their calves, directly toward another observation post that looked just like the last.

"We won't be bothered in here," she assured them. "We're too big. Of course, of course. Oh, Ino. I should have thought of this myself. Unless we should happen to step right on one, but there's very little chance of that. They wait in ambush most of the time, in holes or under rocks."

"They?" Injury and effort were taking toll on Claus. He leaned on Jenny's shoulder now.

Glenna glanced back impatiently. "Mantis shrimp is the common name. They're stomatopods, actually."

"Shrimp?" The dazed query was so soft that she may not have heard it.

A minute later they were squeezed aboard the station and could rest again. Above, clean morning clouds were building to enormous height, clouds that might have formed in the unbreathed air of Earth five hundred million years before.

"Claus," Jen asked, when both of them had caught their breath a little, "what were you saying a while ago, about circling back to the house?"

"It's this way," he said, and paused to organize his thoughts. "We've been running to nowhere, because there's nowhere on this world we can get help. *But the berserkers can't know that.* I'm assuming they haven't scouted the whole planet, but just crash-landed on it. For all they know, there's another colony of humans just down the coast. Maybe a town, with lots of people, aircraft, weapons . . . so for them it's an absolute priority to cut us off before we can give a warning. Therefore every one of their units must be committed to the chase. And if we can once get through them or around them, we can outrun them home, to vehicles and guns and food and water. How we get through them or around them I haven't figured out yet. But I don't see any other way."

"We'll see," said Glenna. Jen held his hand, and looked at him as if his idea might be reasonable. A distracting raindrop hit him on the face, and suddenly a shower was spattering the pond. With open mouths the three survivors caught what drops they could. They tried spreading Jenny's robe out to catch more, but the rain stopped before the cloth was wet.

"Here they come," Glenna informed them, shading her eyes from re-emergent sun. She started tuning up the observing gear aboard the station.

Claus counted brown saucer-shapes dropping into the pond. Only nineteen, after all.

"Again, I can't find them with the sonar," Glenna muttered. "We'll try the television—there."

A berserker unit—for all the watching humans could tell, it was the same one that the shark had swallowed—was centimetering its tireless way toward them, walking the bottom in shallow, sunlit water. Death was walking. A living thing might run more quickly, for a time, but life would tire. Or let life oppose it, if life would. Already it had walked through a shark, as easily as traversing a mass of seaweed.

"There," Glenna breathed again. The advancing enemy had detoured slightly around a rock, and a moment later a dancing ripple of movement had emerged from hiding somewhere to follow in its path. The pursuer's score or so of tiny legs supported in flowing motion a soft-looking, roughly segmented tubular body. Its sinuous length was about the same as the enemy machine's diameter, but in contrast the follower was aglow with life, gold marked in detail with red and green and brown, like banners carried forward above an advancing column. Long antennae waved as if for balance above bulbous, short-stalked eyes. And underneath the eyes a coil of heavy forelimbs rested, not used for locomotion.

"*Odonodactylus syllarus*," Glenna murmured. "Not the biggest species—but maybe big enough."

"What are they?" Jen's voice was a prayerful whisper.

"Well, predators . . ."

The berserker, intent on its own prey, ignored the

animate ripple that was overtaking it, until the smasher
had closed almost to contact range. The machine
paused then, and started to turn.

Before it had rotated itself more than halfway its
brown body was visibly jerked forward, under some
striking impetus from the smasher too fast for human
eyes to follow. The *krak!* of it came clearly through
the audio pickup. Even before the berserker had
regained its balance, it put forth a tearing-claw like
that which had opened the shark's gut from inside.

Again the invisible impact flicked from a finger-
length away. At each spot where one of the berserker's feet touched bottom, a tiny spurt of sand jumped
up with the transmitted shock. Its tearing claw now
dangled uselessly, hard ceramic cracked clean across.

"I've never measured a faster movement by anything that lives. They strike with special dactyls—
well, with their elbows, you might say. They feed
primarily on hard-shelled crabs and clams and snails.
That was just a little one, that Ino gave you as a joke.
One as long as my hand can hit something like a
four-millimeter bullet—and some of these are longer."

Another hungry smasher was now coming swift
upon the track of the brown, shelled thing that looked
so like a crab. The second smasher's eyes moved on
their stalks, calculating distance. It was evidently of a
different species than the first, being somewhat larger
and of a variant coloration. Even as the berserker,
which had just put out another tool, sharp and wiry,
and cut its first assailant neatly in half, turned back,
Claus saw—or almost saw or imagined that he saw—
the newcomer's longest pair of forelimbs unfold and
return. Again grains of sand beneath the two bodies,
living and unliving, jumped from the bottom. With

the concussion white radii of fracture sprang out across a hard, brown surface . . .

Four minutes later the three humans were still watching, in near-perfect silence. A steady barrage of *kraks*, from every region of the pond, were echoing through the audio pickups. The video screen still showed the progress of the first individual combat.

"People sometimes talk about sharks as being aggressive, as terrible killing machines. Gram for gram, I don't think they're at all in the same class."

The smashing stomatopod, incongruously shrimplike, gripping with its six barb-studded smaller forelimbs the ruined casing of its victim—from which a single ceramic walking-limb still thrashed—began to drag it back to the rock from which its ambush had been launched. Once there, it propped the interstellar terror in place, a Lilliputian monster blacksmith arranging metal against anvil. At the next strike, imaginable if not visible as a double backhand snap from the fists of a karate master, fragments of tough casing literally flew through the water, mixed now with a spill of delicate components. What, no soft, delicious meat in sight as yet? Then *smash* again . . .

An hour after the audio pickups had reported their last *krak*, the three humans walked toward home, unmolested through the shallows and along a shore where no brown saucers moved.

When Ino had been brought home, and Claus's hand seen to, the house was searched for enemy survivors. Guns were got out, and the great gates in the sand-walls closed to be on the safe side. Then the two young people sent Glenna to a sedated rest.

Her voice was dazed, and softly, infinitely tired. "Tomorrow we'll feed them, something real."

"This afternoon," said Claus. "When you wake up. Show me what to do."

"Look at this," called Jen a minute later, from the common room.

One wall of the smallest aquarium had been shattered outward. Its tough glass lay sharded on the carpet, along with a large stain of water and the soft body of a small creature, escaped and dead.

Jen picked it up. It was much smaller than its cousins out in the pond, but now she could not mistake the shape, even curled loosely in her palm.

Her husband came in and looked over her shoulder. "Glenna's still muttering. She just told me they can stab, too, if they sense soft meat in contact. Spear-tips on their smashers when they unfold them all the way. So you couldn't hold him like that if he was still alive." Claus's voice broke suddenly, in a delayed reaction.

"Oh, yes I could." Jen's voice too. "Oh, yes I could indeed."

As I said before, most imtelligent creatures avoid war, shun violence. Yet eternal must our gratitude be, to those whose very games are bitter conflict. Grateful, even as we wonder at their hardness—and at the tenderness that may dwell at the same time in the same heart.

THE GAME

Khees rarely looked at the overseers' towers without seeing in them a fanciful resemblance to chess rooks. Instead of four, there were six great rooks here, each one standing on its own corner of a vast patchwork territory of lifeless land; and the patched land, busy with friendly machines, still obscured here and there by blotches of poison mist borne in the thinned and ruined air, was not divided into regular squares; some kind of fairy chess instead of the regular variety. His imaginative thoughts about the towers had not, in the six months he had been on planet Maximus, ever got much farther than this point. Chess was not Khees' great game, and he knew little of its history.

Today he was conducting an informal tour of the rehabilitation project for Adrienne, who had just arrived on-world, and whom he had not seen in over two standard years. At the moment they were outside, wearing dust-repellent jackets and special breathing masks.

"Actually the capital stood more than a thousand

kilometers from here, before the attack. But this will be a finer site in several ways for the new city, so we decided to put the monument here as well."

"That was a good idea. Yours?" It was marvelously flattering, and more than that, the attention that Adrienne was giving him today.

He chuckled. "I'm not sure. We talk things over a great deal." Khees and twenty other people had been here for half a year, overseeing an army of machines employed in starting to undo the devastation wrought by the raiding berserker fleet in an hour or so, a little more than a standard year ago, "Let's go inside again. In here we have the first of our new atmosphere."

They passed through an airlock into a great, inflated, transparent structure, where they could remove the masks that had protected them against the poison residues of the attack, which still maintained an uncanny lifelessness across the open atmosphere. It was not only human life against which the berserkers fought; the commands built into those unliving killers by their ancient and unknown programmers decreed that all life must be destroyed. For many thousands of years the berserkers had ranged the galaxy, replicating themselves, designing new machines as needed, always methodically killing. And now, for a thousand years and more, Earth-descended humanity, dispersed on more than a hundred worlds, had fought against them.

Inside, Adrienne tossed her mask into a rack and looked about, shaking out long hair of fiery red with a brisk twisting of her slender neck. "Enormous," she remarked. The inflated dome of clear plastic, that from outside had seemed so tall, looked flat when seen from inside, so long and broad was it in relation to its height. Almost a kilometer away, beyond a pleasant view of green-fringed paths and ponds, the half-finished monument rose, remaining truncated at the top until the atmosphere had been restored and the confining plastic dome could be removed. SACRED TO THE MEMORY OF, words said across the monument's front, and then a blankness. Khees, whose job mostly involved other matters, didn't know just how it was going to look when finished. Half a million dead, all the citizens of Maximus who had stayed behind to fight, would provide an impressive number of names to fit in, even if not all of them were known.

"And beautiful," Adrienne concluded, completing her first look round the place. "You're doing a fine job here, Khees."

"This will be the central park of the new capital someday. It isn't my project, though. The machines I oversee are working thirty and forty kilometers away."

"I meant all of you who work here," said Adrienne quickly. Was there just a little regret in her voice, as if she wished she could credit him with the park?

She took his arm and they walked along a path. A few Earthbirds, singing, flew overhead. In the distance a pair of Space Marine officers were approaching from the direction of the monument, uniforms immaculate, weapons slung on shoulders as required for full-dress ceremonies.

Adrienne said: "So, down there at the other end is obviously where the Chief is going to lay the wreath. Where will he enter the dome, though? From here it would be too long a walk. We want to control the time factor as much as possible." She was thinking aloud, asking herself the question; it was one of the problems that she, as a member of the advance landing party charged with seeing that the planned ceremony ran smoothly, was going to have to answer.

Khees ran a nervous hand through his own curly black hair. "So, how is it working for the great man?"

"The Chief? He really is, you know."

"I don't suppose you can be elected to lead the Ten Planets without some ability. The war has certainly gone better since he's been in office."

"Oh, he has leadership ability, of course. But I meant humanly great. I suppose the two often go together. He really does care about people. These wreath-laying trips of his to all the battle sites are not just for show. He had tears in his eyes at the last ceremony; I saw them. But how is it with your job, Khees?"

"All right." He shrugged. "A lot of people are a lot worse off. I'm not out in the front line fighting berserkers."

"Still, I don't suppose you get much chance to do what you like best."

Now he looked at her carefully. "No. Actually, no chance at all."

"One of the Marine officers who came in the advance party with me has a minor master's rating. When he found out that I knew you—he already knew you were here—he begged me to see if I could get you to play a game."

"A minor master? Who?"

Adrienne sighed faintly. "I thought that'd catch your interest. His name's Barkro. I didn't ask his numerical rating—I suppose I should have realized you'd want to take that into consideration."

He had—as so often in the past—the feeling that the more he talked with Adrienne, the farther apart the two of them got. "Oh, I'll give him a game. That is, if we can come up with six players—I doubt he'd be interested in any lesser variations. Are you going to play, too?"

She smiled and took his hand. "Why not? I won't have much work to do. And an old boyfriend of mine once taught me how. He even claimed that I had the potential to be pretty good at it someday."

"If you practiced enough, I said. And if you could eliminate a little psychological block or two." Now he was holding both her hands and smiling back at her. On first seeing her an hour ago it had hit him, how much he'd really missed her. And now minute by minute the feeling was growing stronger.

"Well sir, I didn't think my psychological block was all that terrible."

"There *was* something about it rather nice, from my own point of view."

And shortly they were walking on again. She said: "I haven't had the time for any practice at The Game . . . speaking of time, though, are we even going to have enough of it to play? I mean, all of us in the Chief's party are going to be lifting off again just about twelve hours from now."

He calculated. "Let's see—LeBon and Narret will play, I'm sure. One more—Jon Via, probably. Trouble is, most of us who will want to play are going to be at least nominally on duty much of the time. We do six hour shifts, alone in the towers, as a rule . . . what time will the Chief's shuttle land?"

"About ten hours from now."

"Once he lands we'll all be busy—no way out of that."

"Can't you trade shifts with non-players?"

Khees grimaced mildly. "I don't think so. We're short-handed right now, with a bunch of people out on the frontier with our boss, and they won't be back until just about the time the Chief comes down. No real reason we can't play while we're on duty in the towers, though. It's not that demanding a job most of the time. Only reason the towers have to be manned at all is that early on here we had a couple of accidents, and now the Boss insists on having permanent observation posts where human eyes can get a direct overall view of the project, at least a good part of the time."

"What do you do on the night shift?"

He grinned. "The best we can."

"Your machines are not as self-sufficient as they could be, I gather."

"It's the old problem." With the example of the berserkers constantly in mind, human beings on all worlds were afraid to give their own machines, however benignly programmed, nearly as much in the way of general intelligence and self-sufficiency as technology allowed.

"In the Game, will we use the honor system as regards computer help?"

"Of course." Khees felt a little disappointed, almost injured, by the question. If you were serious enough about the Game to play it well, you weren't going to cheat, certainly not in that crude a sense. Would an athlete tie servolifters to his wrists, and then take pride in winning a weight contest?

"Silly of me to ask . . ."

"It's all right. Look, Ade, I've got to get back up in my tower. The Boss just might call in checking up; he takes his overseers' duties rather seriously."

"Then he won't approve of a Game during duty hours."

"What he doesn't know won't hurt him."

"What if he tunes in his radio later and hears us playing?"

"We'll use light-beam communication, tower to tower. I'll start getting things set up for play. Want to come along? That'll be against regulations also, but . . ."

"Love to, but I have a thing or two I must get done myself before we start frittering our time. Where am I going to be when we play?"

"Best thing will be to put you in an unused tower . . . we can manage that. Be talking to you soon."

The Game had different names in different human languages. To Khees, in his innermost thoughts, it often had no name at all. Do fish have names for water? Anyway, very few people on his home world had been game-minded, and there it had a name that translated into English bluntly as War-Without-Blood. Since he had come to know The Game, Khees had always preferred it to the "real" world, in which the elder members of his family (he had grown up in that kind of reality) assigned jobs to the younger, himself included.

"Oh, I'm not afraid of work, Uncle. And I can see it's my duty as a citizen and all that to help out. But I really don't want ten million people looking to me for answers every day."

"You could have even more people than that looking up to you." (Which perhaps Khees had already, counting all the Game fans across the Earth-colonized corner of the Galaxy. But on his homeworld, none of that was ever completely real.) "You have a brilliant mind, my boy, and it beats me how you can be content to use it for nothing more than . . . than . . ."

"Well sir, how can you be content to use your own intelligence at nothing more than shuffling matter around? Who cares if the population of Toxx can build their houses fifteen meters tall next year or only ten?"

That earned Khees a stern avuncular glare. "Well, the population of Toxx might care! In fact, most of them do. Housing construction is something . . . something very worthwhile. Rewarding."

"For you. Not me. I just don't care. I couldn't."

And this was after they had sent him to a fine engineering school. The old man glared harder. Then he found a stronger move to make. "Maybe you can find it in you to care how deep people are able to dig their shelters, against the day when the berserkers come again. Now there's a *real* problem for you. Hey?"

"Other people are just as smart as I am about that kind of problem, and a lot more anxious to tackle it. Putting someone like me in charge of any military matters would not be a wise move."

"If only it were part of some game, Khees, you'd solve it brilliantly." His uncle coughed morosely. As long as, his unstated theory ran, real people's lives were not involved.

"Are you saying, then, that every brilliant person must be a fortifications expert? Why not a strategist?"

"Now, there's another—"

"Why not a doctor? Then we could always be ready to treat each other's wounds, in case of sudden attack or accident."

Why not a lawyer? He could certainly play the game of argument, varying tactics to suit opponents, sending most of them retreating in confusion. Opponent must totter two spaces backward, according to the Argument Results Calculator. Even if Opponent had started out with what looked like a real advantage in his logic. Logic was only one part of even the most logical of human games.

But eventually Khees wearied of the arguing, and so did they. A compromise was reached; and here he was now, doing a real-world job, and even a job that carried a fair amount of status in society. The family politicians had, among them, seen to that.

The elevator opened silently. Ahead, the door to the overseer's room atop Khees' own chess rook stood ajar as usual, and he walked in. Great sealed windows viewed the patchwork land two hundred meters down, the thin-aired, purple sky, the five other towers that stood no more than a kilometer or two away, heads just level with the misty flatness of horizon.

"Anything going on, Kara?"

"Booby traps again." The woman he was relieving looked up from her panels with a brief smile. "Double one, this time." In one sense, Maximus had not yet been completely reconquered from the berserkers. "The second went off and did some damage to the engineer machines while they were clearing out the first."

Khees stood beside her, scanning the printouts and the panels. "Haven't had booby traps for a while. Doesn't look too bad, though, hey? Anything else?"

"No." Like everyone else in the permanent party, Kara was anxious to have her chance to socialize with the visitors in the brief time they were on-world.

"Well, this doesn't look too hard to handle. Go on, take off."

Kara was hardly out the door before a communicator chimed. Radio brought in the voice of the robot foreman on Khees' sector of the distant frontier of work. The robot was evidently speaking from the scene of the latest accident.

"Overseer, I request that an aircar be sent out here immediately from Central." Its mechanical voice was deep and pleasant, as unlike as it could be made from the voices that berserkers usually took to themselves when they put on the habit of human speech.

"An aircar. What for?"

"Part JS-828 in the forward limb assembly of a workrobot Type Six is broken. The workrobot is otherwise essentially undamaged, and can be speedily returned to duty if a replacement part is sent out."

Khees was already punching at his computer console to get a look at the inventory of spare parts. He thought he knew what he would find, and he was right. A similar part had been broken in a freak accident ten days ago, and the stock of replacements was now down to zero. He so informed his foreman. "We'll bring in the damaged piece, then, and the shop can decide whether to try to fix it, or produce a new one, or wait and hope we get another on the next shipment in."

"Is then the aircar to be sent?"

Khees, on the verge of turning his mind to something else, paused. The video screen was blank, since the Boss believed that screens were distracting when not absolutely necessary, but he stared at it anyway. "No, a groundcar will come, as usual for repairs. Perhaps the mobile repair machine can fix the workrobot on the spot."

"It appears to me that it will not." The robot foreman's permanently jovial tones made the announcement of bad news sound impertinent. Maybe it was only that, but Khees thought the damned thing sounded odd today.

"You're not qualified to judge," he told it. "The groundcar's coming." Good roads had been laid as far as that work area; the difference in time between ground transport and air would be minimal. "Meanwhile proceed with the programmed job as best you can."

"Orders understood. Proceeding."

Khees switched off that communicator, and turned to another, the tight light-beam that could be used for private talk among the towers.

And now, he thought. The Game.

It was certainly not chess, though its inventor had been one of the great chess masters of the very late twentieth century. Like any other board game, it could be played by a computer, and its inventor had in fact used one of the most advanced computer systems of his day to help design it. He had sought to create a game that could be played by a computer but not analyzed by one; not for The Game were the endless labyrinths of opening theory that now made learning chess more of a burden than a joy.

Having six players helped make The Game resistant to analysis, and was no longer much of a drawback to practical play. By the close of the twentieth century there were on old Earth a lot of bright people with a lot of spare time and a taste for games. But what really foiled computer analysis, outside of actual play, was the sophisticated addition of chance to the Game; whatever moves a computer came up with for a particular contest would probably be useless in any other. Openings tended to be wild; it was proverbial that you had to be either good or lucky to survive the opening at all, and it was much better to be both. Khees had not failed to survive an opening in serious play since his first tournament, a startling (to him) number of years ago.

The players were in place in their several towers, and the preliminaries were over; play began. Adrienne and Barkro had been installed in towers otherwise unused at the moment. Jon Via, LeBon, and Narret all signalled ready, their light-beams winking dully from the horizon.

Play was shown on the large video screen normally reserved for emergencies; the pictured board was a simulation of a space war, stylized to the point of complete unrealism, the six fleets showing as points or bars of different colors. In the opening moves, Khees played conservatively, content to survive the buffetings of chance. He parried deadly threats when they appeared, and otherwise tried nothing more ambitious than a small improvement of position here, the mobilization of a new squadron there, saving his efforts for the middle game, when chance would be less important. Barkro justified Adrienne's estimate of his skill by adopting the same general course. Adrienne herself, a basically good player but not of master strength, was given advantage by luck in the early moves, and seemed daringly determined to make the most of it. She was off at once on a flashy, aggressive campaign, threatening Khees, threatening Via. If her good luck held for another half-dozen moves she might have a won game before the opening was fairly over. She was a brilliant woman in most fields of mental endeavor; and if it were not for a certain little quirk or two, she could learn to be brilliant in this as well . . .

The other players performed generally like the strong amateurs they were. LeBon launched a well-planned though premature attack on Adrienne, thinking evidently that if he waited she was only going to get stronger, and no doubt expecting he would get support from Khees. Open diplomacy was not part of The Game, but tacit agreements and understandings were.

Khees moved in turn, without having to take much thought. He had plenty of time between moves to go through the undemanding routine of an overseer's watch, observing what he could of his distant machinery with binoculars, eyeing the panels and printers that brought more precise information in from the frontier. He would not have cared to enter a championship tournament in his present rusty and unpracticed state; years had now passed since he had played against serious opposition. But in this game he thought himself in more danger of boredom than of losing—except for Barkro, of course, they didn't give out master's ratings, even low ones, lightly. Barkro was the one to watch, and to really play against.

A good thing, too, that he could manage without perfect concentration, for this was turning out to be a day of oddities on the job. Here, for example, came the groundcar back from the frontier, presumably carrying the damaged part—and it stopped and hesitated and made false starts after entering the Central complex, as if its directing computer could have somehow become confused about which tunnel-mouth of the underground works would lead it to the proper repair shop.

Could someone have set up a ploy involving robots and groundcars to distract him from the Game by making him think that something regarding the work in his sector was really going wrong? He began to watch his panels very carefully.

On the game board, through the next few turns, Adrienne's power was still augmented by moderately good luck. Luck would mean less and less, though, as the Game progressed. LeBon, pounced on from behind, was all but out. Could LeBon be the one to gimmick groundcars? No. And Adrienne and Barkro were visitors, lacking the expertise. Jon Via was serious enough about winning, and knowledgeable enough. But . . .

Another round of moves, another, and now an expert stranger would have been convinced that Adrienne was going to win. Barkro's forces were still mainly intact, but he was beaten. Khees had suddenly struck at him instead of at Adrienne. The visiting master was doubtless a bit stunned, unable to believe that Khees was going to throw the game so blatantly to his old girl friend—which of course was not what Khees had in mind at all. On a Game board, Khees would have smashed his own mother into a corner just as soon as the best chance came to do it. If you want to be nice, and sociable, play something else . . .

Now they were all waiting for Adrienne's next move, which was quite slow in coming. Khees smiled a little to himself.

"Adrienne? We're waiting for your move." That voice on the light-beam net among the towers was Barkro's, sounding half impatient, half sulky with the way he thought the Game was going.

Shortly her move came on the board. Coldly logical, completely crushing.

Khees' smile vanished. Wrong . . . impulsively he opened the microphone before him. "Adrienne . . ."

"What?" Her answering voice was cold, too, and he thought it had a distracted sound. A day for unusual voices, among its other oddities.

And on the panel to his right, three indicators showed minor troubles out on his section of the frontier. Things that the foreman should be taking care of. Maybe the foreman would get to them soon, he told himself.

Khees and the other players moved through the round, and Adrienne moved again. With sudden clarity Khees understood. He felt a weakness in the knees, not unlike that he had known in some tournaments, but more intense. He faced certain and utter defeat.

Or almost. Logic said loss, but there were still intangibles. There might be one, just one, more chance for the right move . . .

The sound of the opening of the door of her tower room, soft though it was, startled Adrienne. Why would anyone come up here now—?

She turned. Before there was time for fear the silent speed-blurred rush of something vaguely manlike in size and shape, but embodying a flow of metal and power that could not possibly be human, culminated in cold grippers touching her throat and then each of her limbs in turn.

By the time she would have screamed it was too late. She could not talk, could barely breathe; something small but weighty clung to her throat after the machine had set her down in a corner, propped in an angle of wall. She could move her head, enough to look down at herself. To each of her paralyzed arms and legs a thing that looked like a small metal leech was now attached.

Berserker . . .

When screaming failed, she willed herself to faint. That failed also.

The man-sized thing, ignoring her now, began a quick scanning of the tower's instruments, of which only the Game board screen and the lightbeam communicator were functioning. In seconds it had completed this inspection. With a snapping sound it now opened its own torso, and brought out a small stand which unfolded to support a tube filled with a weighty something. This assembly the berserker erected on a ledge below one of the great windows, adjusting the tube to point downwards at an angle, in the direction of . . .

The monument was down there, at that end of the great plastic dome.

The Chief was on his way . . .

"Adrienne?" The voice coming through the communicator startled her so her half-deadened body almost jumped against the supporting walls. "We're waiting for your move."

If the berserker had been startled too (if in its own electronic way it could be startled), it did not jump, but went at once to the Game-screen. Adrienne had a wild hope that it would not know what The Game was, but her hope was doomed. After five seconds' study it reached out a metal arm to the controls, and moved for her.

Another man's voice, Khees' voice, said into the small room: "Adrienne . . ."

To her absolute horror, what seemed to be her

own voice now issued from the metal creature's throat. "What?"

There was a small pause. "Oh, nothing," Khees replied, dejectedly. And that, it seemed, was that . . .

. . . she looked up from a blur of faintness to find the thing crouched down beside her. Glassy scanners that were not shaped or spaced like human eyes were studying her face.

"Now," it said when she looked up. (And this was surely its preferred voice, this screech that somehow formed itself in distinct words.) "Now you are to provide me with complete details on the itinerary of the visit here of the life-unit which you call the Chief, which serves as Premier of the Ten Planets. If you cooperate you will be spared. If you do not—" Another click, and in one metal hand it showed a small container. "This is nerve acid. One drop instantly penetrates the surface of human skin. It has affinity for living tissues of the sensory system, and it produces in them pain beyond any—"

So silent were the towers' elevators that even the berserker had evidently not heard this one's functioning outside the room's closed door. But now someone was gently, with seeming casualness, trying that door and finding that it was locked.

"Who is it?" It was Adrienne's voice again. And with a swiftness almost unbelievable the machine had crossed the room, was standing just to one side of that closed door. Small projections like gun-muzzles had appeared upon its chest and shoulders, and it poised like a praying mantis, ready to strike with arms of steel.

"Who is it?"

"Message for Adrienne Britton." Some male voice she did not recognize.

"I'm busy."

"Look, lady, do you want this note or do I have to hike all the way back there and tell him you won't take it? It's something about some damn game you're supposed to be playing; he's all upset. Didn't want anyone else to see this or hear it."

"All right. Just hand it in."

Pounding her head against the metal wall, about the only movement she could make, was not going to create enough sound to serve as warning—

The berserker unlocked and opened the door part way. And in the same motion, faster than any human could possibly act or react, it reached forward and outward in a swift grabbing blur—

—and was hurled back, lifted from its feet and flung across the room, held skewered upon a lance of pounding flame. The small room roared with a continuous concussion. The metal body was smashed into the window, where tough plastic cracked and broke but would not yield entirely, and now the chamber filled with outward-rushing fog. Air pressure dropped. Three human figures, masked, in partial armor, tensely crouching, cleared the door. Two of them seemed to be pulled forward by the flaring, jerking weapons in their arms. The third one came for her. The last thing Adrienne saw before the thinning air blanked out her brain was Khees' eyes above a breathing mask . . .

"So some of the Marines' small arms have kinetic sensors now," Khees was saying, walking with her in the park, helping her work out some of the stiffness left in her legs after the metal leeches had been removed. "One of my escort had his weapon set to trigger at anything moving extraordinarily fast—

like a berserker's grabbing arm. Whammo, locks on target and keeps firing until the operator turns it off."

Adrienne shuddered, and squeezed his arm. "You knew it was a berserker," she said, regarding him. "And yet you came for me."

"Walking between two Space Marines. Even so my knees were shaking."

"It might have fired through the door at you, not grabbed."

"We figured that it wanted to be quiet, until the Chief came down and it could get a shot at him. It was a special assassin-machine, of course. They must have thought it a good bet that sooner or later the Chief would show up on Maximus to do his wreath-laying as he has so many other places. So before their raiders left they planted one extra-special booby trap; it must have been monitoring our local radio chatter and it knew when he was coming."

"You knew it was a berserker and yet you came for me. But—how'd you know?"

"Well. There were some strange things going on, with the work machines. Too much of a coincidence, just when the Chief was due. It hit me that an assassin-machine could have taken the place of my foreman, and then come back here to Central in a groundcar I sent out. And where else would it go, to get a good shot at the Chief, but up in one of the towers overlooking the monument? So I hooked up my own computer to play a few moves of the Game for me, and . . ."

"But how did you know that it was in *my* tower?"

"How do you think?" Smiling at her.

Adrienne was smiling too, and at the same time trying not to cry. "My little psychological block. You knew I could never in all my life have brought myself to beat you in The Game."

As life may transmit evil, so machines of great power may hand on good.

WINGS OUT OF SHADOW

In Malori's first and only combat mission the berserker came to him in the image of a priest of the sect into which Malori had been born on the planet Yaty. In a dreamlike vision that was the analogue of a very real combat he saw the robed figure standing tall in a deformed pulpit, eyes flaming with malevolence, lowering arms winglike with the robes they stretched. With their lowering, the lights of the universe were dimming outside the windows of stained glass and Malori was being damned.

Even with his heart pounding under damnation's terror Malori retained sufficient consciousness to remember the real nature of himself and of his adversary and that he was not powerless against him. His dream-feet walked him timelessly toward the pulpit and its demon-priest while all around him the stained glass windows burst, showering him with fragments of sick fear. He walked a crooked path, avoiding the places in the smooth floor where, with quick gestures, the priest created snarling, snapping stone mouths full of teeth. Malori seemed to have unlimited time to decide where to put his feet. *Weapon,*

203

he thought, a surgeon instructing some invisible aide. *Here—in my right hand*.

From those who had survived similar battles he had heard how the inhuman enemy appeared to each in different form, how each human must live the combat through in terms of a unique nightmare. To some a berserker came as a ravening beast, to others as devil or god or man. To still others it was some essence of terror that could never be faced or even seen. The combat was a nightmare experienced while the subconscious ruled, while the waking mind was suppressed by careful electrical pressures on the brain. Eyes and ears were padded shut so that the conscious mind might be more easily suppressed, the mouth plugged to save the tongue from being bitten, the nude body held immobile by the defensive fields that kept it whole against the thousands of gravities that came with each movement of the one-man ship while in combat mode. It was a nightmare from which mere terror could never wake one; waking came only when the fight was over, came only with death or victory or disengagement.

Into Malori's dream-hand there now came a meat cleaver keen as a razor, massive as a guillotine-blade. So huge it was that had it been what it seemed it would have been far too cumbersome to even lift. His uncle's butcher shop on Yaty was gone, with all other human works of that planet. But the cleaver came back to him now, magnified, perfected to suit his need.

He gripped it hard in both hands and advanced. As he drew near the pulpit towered higher. The carved dragon on its front, which should have been an angel, came alive, blasting him with rosy fire.

With a shield that came from nowhere, he parried the splashing flames.

Outside the remnants of the stained glass windows the lights of the universe were almost dead now. Standing at the base of the pulpit, Malori drew back his cleaver as if to strike overhand at the priest who towered above his reach. Then, without any forethought at all, he switched his aim at the top of his backswing and laid the blow crashing against the pulpit's stem. It shook, but resisted stoutly. Damnation came.

Before the devils reached him, though, the energy was draining from the dream. In less than a second of real time it was no more than a fading visual image, a few seconds after that a dying memory. Malori, coming back to consciousness with eyes and ears still sealed, floated in a soothing limbo. Before post-combat fatigue and sensory deprivation could combine to send him into psychosis, attachments on his scalp began to feed his brain with bursts of pins-and-needles noise. It was the safest signal to administer to a brain that might be on the verge of any of a dozen different kinds of madness. The noises made a whitish roaring scattering of light and sound that seemed to fill his head and at the same time somehow outlined for him the positions of his limbs.

His first fully conscious thought: he had just fought a berserker and survived. He had won—or had at least achieved a stand-off—or he would not be here. It was no mean achievement.

Berserkers were like no other foe that Earth-descended human beings had ever faced. They had cunning and intelligence and yet were not alive. Relics of some interstellar war over long ages since, automated machines, warships for the most part, they carried as their basic programming the command to destroy all life wherever it could be found. Yaty was only the latest of many Earth-colonized planets to suffer a berserker attack, and it was among the luckiest; nearly all its people had been successfully evacuated. Malori and others now fought in deep space to protect the *Hope*, one of the enormous evacuation ships. The *Hope* was a sphere several kilometers in diameter, large enough to contain a good proportion of the planet's population stored tier on tier in defense-field stasis. A trickle-relaxation of the fields allowed them to breathe and live with slowed metabolism.

The voyage to a safe sector of the galaxy was going to take several months because most of it, in terms of time spent, was going to be occupied in traversing an outlying arm of the great Taynarus nebula. Here gas and dust were much too thick to let a ship duck out of normal space and travel faster than light. Here even the speeds attainable in normal space were greatly restricted. At thousands of kilometers per second, manned ship or berserker machine could alike be smashed flat against a wisp of gas far more tenuous than human breath.

Taynarus was a wilderness of uncharted plumes and tendrils of dispersed matter, laced through by corridors of relatively empty space. Much of the wilderness was completely shaded by interstellar dust from the light of all the suns outside. Through dark shoals and swamps and tides of nebula the *Hope* and her escort *Judith* fled, and a berserker pack pursued. Some berserkers were even larger than the *Hope*, but those that had taken up this chase were much smaller. In regions of space so thick with matter, a race went to the small as well as to the swift; as the impact cross-section of a ship increased, its maximum practical speed went inexorably down.

The *Hope*, ill-adapted for this chase (in the rush to evacuate, there had been no better choice available) could not expect to outrun the smaller and more maneuverable enemy. Hence the escort carrier *Judith*, trying always to keep herself between *Hope* and the pursuing pack. *Judith* mothered the little fighting ships, spawning them out whenever the enemy came too near, welcoming survivors back when the threat had once again been beaten off. There had been fifteen of the one-man ships when the chase began. Now there were nine.

The noise injections from Malori's life support equipment slowed down, then stopped. His conscious mind once more sat steady on its throne. The gradual relaxation of his defense fields he knew to be a certain sign that he would soon rejoin the world of waking men.

As soon as his fighter, Number Four, had docked itself inside the *Judith* Malori hastened to disconnect himself from the tiny ship's systems. He pulled on a loose coverall and let himself out of the cramped space. A thin man with knobby joints and an awkward step, he hurried along a catwalk through the echoing hangar-like chamber, noting that three or four fighters besides his had already returned and were resting in their cradles. The artificial gravity was quite steady but Malori stumbled and almost fell in his haste to get down the short ladder to the operations deck.

Petrovich, commander of the *Judith*, a bulky, iron-faced man of middle height, was on the deck apparently waiting for him.

"Did—did I make my kill?" Malori stuttered eagerly as he came hurrying up. The forms of military address were little observed aboard the *Judith*, as a rule, and Malori was really a civilian anyway. That he had been allowed to take out a fighter at all was a mark of the commander's desperation.

Scowling, Petrovich answered bluntly. "Malori, you're a disaster in one of these ships. Haven't the mind for it at all."

The world turned a little gray in front of Malori. He hadn't understood until this moment just how important to him certain dreams of glory were. He could find only weak and awkward words. "But . . . I thought I did all right." He tried to recall his combat-nightmare. Something about a church.

"Two people had to divert their ships from their original combat objectives to rescue you. I've already seen their gun-camera tapes. You had Number Four just sparring around with that berserker as if you had no intention of doing it any damage at all." Petrovich looked at him more closely, shrugged, and softened his voice somewhat. "I'm not trying to chew you out, you weren't even aware of what was happening, of course. I'm just stating facts. Thank probability the *Hope* is twenty AU deep in a formaldehyde cloud up ahead. If she'd been in an exposed position just now they would have got her."

"But—" Malori tried to begin an argument but the commander simply walked away. More fighters were coming in. Locks sighed and cradles clanged, and Petrovich had plenty of more important things to do than stand here arguing with him. Malori stood there alone for a few moments, feeling deflated and defeated and diminished. Involuntarily he cast a yearning glance back at Number Four. It was a short, windowless cylinder, not much more than a man's height in diameter, resting in its metal cradle while technicians worked about it. The stubby main laser nozzle, still hot from firing, was sending up a wisp of smoke now that it was back in atmosphere. There was his two-handed cleaver.

No man could direct a ship or a weapon with anything like the competence of a good machine. The creeping slowness of human nerve impulses and of conscious thought disqualified humans from maintaining direct control of their ships in any space fight against berserkers. But the human subconscious was not so limited. Certain of its processes could not be correlated with any specific synaptic activity within the brain, and some theorists held that these processes took place outside of time. Most physicists stood aghast at this view—but for space combat it made a useful working hypothesis.

In combat, the berserker computers were coupled with sophisticated randoming devices, to provide the flair, the unpredictability that gained an advantage over an opponent who simply and consistently chose the maneuver statistically most likely to bring success. Men also used computers to drive their ships, but had now gained an edge over the best randomizers by relying once more on their own brains, parts of which were evidently freed of hurry and dwelt outside of time, where even speeding light must be as motionless as carved ice.

There were drawbacks. Some people (including Malori, it now appeared) were simply not suitable for the job, their subconscious minds seemingly uninterested in such temporal matters as life or death. And even in suitable minds the subconscious was subject to great stress. Connection to external computers loaded the mind in some way not yet understood. One after another, human pilots returning from combat were removed from their ships in states of catatonia or hysterical excitement. Sanity might be restored, but the man or woman was worthless thereafter as a combat-computer's teammate. The system was so new that the importance of these drawbacks was just coming to light aboard the *Judith* now. The trained operators of the fighting ships had been used up, and so had their replacements. Thus it was that Ian Malori, historian, and others were sent out, untrained, to fight. But using their minds had bought a little extra time.

From the operations deck Malori went to his small single cabin. He had not eaten for some time, but he was not hungry. He changed clothes and sat in a chair looking at his bunk, looking at his books and tapes and violin, but he did not try to rest or to occupy himself. He expected that he would promptly get a call from Petrovich. Because Petrovich now had nowhere else to turn.

He almost smiled when the communicator chimed, bringing a summons to meet with the commander and other officers at once. Malori acknowledged and set out, taking with him a brown leather-like case about the size of a briefcase but differently shaped, which he selected from several hundred similar cases in a small room adjacent to his cabin. The case he carried was labeled: CRAZY HORSE.

Petrovich looked up as Malori entered the small planning room in which the handful of ship's officers were already gathered around a table. The commander glanced at the case Malori was carrying, and nodded. "It seems we have no choice, historian. We are running out of people, and we are going to have to use your pseudopersonalities. Fortunately we now have the necessary adapters installed in all the fighting ships."

"I think the chances of success are excellent." Malori spoke mildly as he took the seat left vacant for him and set his case out in the middle of the table. "These of course have no real subconscious minds, but as we agreed in our earlier discussions, they will provide more sophisticated randoming devices than are available otherwise. Each has a unique, if artificial, personality."

One of the other officers leaned forward. "Most of us missed these earlier discussions you speak of. Could you fill us in a little?"

"Certainly." Malori cleared his throat. "These personae, as we usually call them, are used in the computer simulation of historical problems. I was able to bring several hundred of them with me from Yaty. Many are models of military men." He put his hand on the case before him. "This is a reconstruction of the personality of one of the most able cavalry leaders on ancient Earth. It's not one of the group we have selected to try first in combat, I just brought it along to demonstrate the interior structure and design for any of you who are interested. Each persona contains about four million sheets of two-dimensional matter."

Another officer raised a hand. "How can you accurately reconstruct the personality of someone who must have died long before any kind of direct recording techniques were available?"

"We can't be positive of accuracy, of course. We have only historical records to go by, and what we deduce from computer simulations of the era. These are only models. But they should perform in combat as in the historical studies for which they were made. Their choices should reflect basic aggressiveness, determination—"

The totally unexpected sound of an explosion brought the assembled officers as one body to their feet. Petrovich, reacting very fast, still had time only to get clear of his chair before a second and much louder blast resounded through the ship. Malori himself was almost at the door, heading for his battle station, when the third explosion came. It sounded like the end of the galaxy, and he was aware that furniture was flying, that the bulkheads around the meeting room were caving in. Malori had one clear, calm thought about the unfairness of his coming death, and then for a time he ceased to think at all.

Coming back was a slow unpleasant process. He knew *Judith* was not totally wrecked for he still breathed, and the artificial gravity still held him sprawled out against the deck. It might have been pleasing to find the gravity gone, for his body was one vast, throbbing ache, a pattern of radiated pain from a center somewhere inside his skull. He did not want to pin down the source any more closely than that. To even imagine touching his own head was painful.

At last the urgency of finding out what was going on overcame the fear of pain and he raised his head and probed it. There was a large lump just above his forehead, and smaller injuries about his face where blood had dried. He must have been out for some time.

The meeting room was ruined, shattered, littered with debris. There was a crumpled body that must be dead, and there another, and another, mixed in with the furniture. Was he the only survivor? One bulkhead had been torn wide open, and the planning table was demolished. And what was that large, unfamiliar piece of machinery standing at the other end of the room? Big as a tall filing cabinet, but far more intricate. There was something peculiar about its legs, as if they might be movable . . .

Malori froze in abject terror, because the thing did move, swiveling a complex of turrets and lenses at him, and he understood that he was seeing and being seen by a functional berserker machine. It was one of the small ones, used for boarding and operating captured human ships.

"Come here," the machine said. It had a squeaky, ludicrous parody of a human voice, recorded syllables of captives' voices stuck together electronically and played back. "The badlife has awakened."

Malori in his great fear thought that the words were directed at him but he could not move. Then, stepping through the hole in the bulkhead, came a man Malori had never seen before—a shaggy and filthy man wearing a grimy coverall that might once have been part of some military uniform.

"I see he has, sir," the man said to the machine. He spoke the standard interstellar language in a ragged voice that bore traces of a cultivated accent. He took a step closer to Malori. "Can you understand me, there?"

Malori grunted something, tried to nod, pulled himself up slowly into an awkward sitting position.

"The question is," the man continued, coming a little closer still, "how d'you want it later, easy or hard? When it comes to your finishing up, I mean. I decided a long time ago that I want mine quick and easy, and not too soon. Also that I still want to have some fun here and there along the way."

Despite the fierce pain in his head, Malori was thinking now, and beginning to understand. There was a name for humans like the man before him, who went along more or less willingly with the berserker machines. A word coined by the machines themselves. But at the moment Malori was not going to speak that name.

"I want it easy," was all he said, and blinked his eyes and tried to rub his neck against the pain.

The man looked him over in silence a little longer. "All right," he said then. Turning back to the machine, he added in a different, humble voice: "I can easily dominate this injured badlife. There will be no problems if you leave us here alone."

The machine turned one metal-cased lens toward its servant. "Remember," it vocalized, "the auxiliaries must be made ready. Time grows short. Failure will bring unpleasant stimuli."

"I will remember, sir." The man was humble and sincere. The machine looked at both of them a few moments longer and then departed, metal legs flowing suddenly into a precise and almost graceful walk. Shortly after, Malori heard the familiar sound of an airlock cycling.

"We're alone now," the man said, looking down at him. "If you want a name for me you can call me Greenleaf. Want to try to fight me? If so, let's get it over with." He was not much bigger than Malori but his hands were huge and he looked hard and very capable despite his ragged filthiness. "All right, that's a smart choice. You know, you're actually a lucky man, though you don't realize it yet. Berserkers aren't like the other masters that men have—not like the governments and parties and corporations and causes that use you up and then just let you drop and drag away. No, when the machines run out of uses for you they'll finish you off quickly and cleanly—if you've served well. I know, I've seen 'em do it that way with other humans. No reason why they shouldn't. All they want is for us to die, not suffer."

Malori said nothing. He thought perhaps he would be able to stand up soon.

Greenleaf (the name seemed so inappropriate that Malori thought it probably real) made some adjustment on a small device that he had taken from a pocket and was holding almost concealed in one large hand. He asked: "How many escort carriers besides this one are trying to protect the *Hope?*"

"I don't know," Malori lied. There had been only the *Judith*.

"What is your name?" The bigger man was still looking at the device in his hand.

"Ian Malori."

Greenleaf nodded, and without showing any particular emotion in his face took two steps forward and kicked Malori in the belly, precisely and with brutal power.

"That was for trying to lie to me, Ian Malori," said his captor's voice, heard dimly from somewhere above as Malori groveled on the deck, trying to breathe again. "Understand that I am infallibly able to tell when you are lying. Now, how many escort carriers are there?"

In time Malori could sit up again, and choke out words. "Only this one." Whether Greenleaf had a real lie detector, or was only trying to make it appear so by asking questions whose answers he already knew, Malori decided that from now on he would speak the literal truth as scrupulously as possible. A few more kicks like that and he would be helpless and useless and the machines would kill him. He discovered that he was by no means ready to abandon his life.

"What was your position on the crew, Malori?"

"I'm a civilian."

"What sort?"

"An historian."

"And why are you here?"

Malori started to try to get to his feet, then decided there was nothing to be gained by the struggle and stayed sitting on the deck. If he ever let himself dwell on his situation for a moment he would be too hideously afraid to think coherently. "There was a project . . . you see, I brought with me from Yaty a number of what we call historical models—blocks of programmed responses we use in historical research."

"I remember hearing about some such things. What was the project you mentioned?"

"Trying to use the personae of military men as randomizers for the combat computers on the one-man ships."

"Aha." Greenleaf squatted, supple and poised for all his raunchy look. "How do they work in combat? Better than a live pilot's subconscious mind? The machines know all about *that*."

"We never had a chance to try. Are the rest of the crew here all dead?"

Greenleaf nodded casually. "It wasn't a hard boarding. There must have been a failure in your automatic defenses. I'm glad to find one man alive and smart enough to cooperate. It'll help me in my career." He glanced at an expensive chronometer strapped to his dirty wrist. "Stand up, Ian Malori. There's work to do."

Malori got up and followed the other toward the operations deck.

"The machines and I have been looking around, Malori. These nine little fighting ships you still have on board are just too good to be wasted. The machines are sure of catching the *Hope* now, but she'll have automatic defenses, probably a lot tougher than this tub's were. The machines have taken a lot of casualties on this chase so they mean to use these nine little ships as auxiliary troops—no doubt you have some knowledge of military history?"

"Some." The answer was perhaps an understatement, but it seemed to pass as truth. The lie detector, if it was one, had been put away. But Malori would still take no more chances than he must.

"Then you probably know how some of the generals of old Earth used their auxiliaries. Drove them on ahead of the main force of trusted troops, where they could be killed if they tried to retreat, and were also the first to be used up against the enemy."

Arriving on the operations deck, Malori saw few signs of damage. Nine tough little ships waited in their launching cradles, re-armed and refueled for combat. All that would have been taken care of within minutes of their return from their last mission.

"Malori, from looking at these ships' controls while you were unconscious, I gather that there's no fully automatic mode in which they can be operated."

"Right. There has to be some controlling mind, or randomizer, connected on board."

"You and I are going to get them out as berserker auxiliaries, Ian Malori." Greenleaf glanced at his timepiece again. "We have less than an hour to think of a

good way and only a few hours more to complete the
job. The faster the better. If we delay we are going
to be made to suffer for it." He seemed almost to
relish the thought. "What do you suggest we do?"

Malori opened his mouth as if to speak, and then
did not.

Greenleaf said: "Installing any of your military personae is of course out of the question, as they might
not submit well to being driven forward like mere
cannon fodder. I assume they are leaders of some
kind. But have you perhaps any of these personae
from different fields, of a more docile nature?"

Malori, sagging against the operations officer's empty
combat chair, forced himself to think very carefully
before he spoke. "As it happens, there are some
personae aboard in which I have a special personal
interest. Come."

With the other following closely, Malori led the
way to his small bachelor cabin. Somehow it was
astonishing that nothing had been changed inside.
There on the bunk was his violin, and on the table
were his music tapes and a few books. And here,
stacked neatly in their leather-like curved cases, were
some of the personae that he liked best to study.

Malori lifted the top case from the stack. "This
man was a violinist, as I like to think I am. His name
would probably mean nothing to you."

"Musicology was never my field. But tell me more."

"He was an Earthman, who lived in the twentieth
century CE—quite a religious man, too, as I understand. We can plug the persona in and ask it what it
thinks of fighting, if you are suspicious."

"We had better do that." When Malori had shown
him the proper receptacle beside the cabin's small
computer console, Greenleaf snapped the connec-

tions together himself. "How does one communicate with it?"

"Just talk."

Greenleaf spoke sharply toward the leather-like case. "Your name?"

"Albert Ball." The voice that answered from the console speaker sounded more human by far than the berserker's had.

"How does the thought of getting into a fight strike you, Albert?"

"A detestable idea."

"Will you play the violin for us?"

"Gladly." But no music followed.

Malori put in: "More connections are necessary if you want actual music."

"I don't think we'll need that." Greenleaf unplugged the Albert Ball unit and began to look through the stack of others, frowning at unfamiliar names. There were twelve or fifteen cases in all. "Who are these?"

"Albert Ball's contemporaries. Performers who shared his profession." Malori let himself sink down on the bunk for a few moments' rest. He was not far from fainting. Then he went to stand with Greenleaf beside the stack of personae. "This is a model of Edward Mannock, who was blind in one eye and could never have passed the physical examination necessary to serve in any military force of his time." He pointed to another. "This man served briefly in the cavalry, as I recall, but he kept getting thrown from his horse and was soon relegated to gathering supplies. And this one was a frail, tubercular youth who died at twenty-three standard years of age."

Greenleaf gave up looking at the cases and turned to size up Malori once again. Malori could feel his battered stomach muscles trying to contract, anticipating another violent impact. It would be too much, it was going to kill him if it came like that again . . .

"All right." Greenleaf was frowning, checking his chronometer yet again. Then he looked up with a little smile. Oddly, the smile made him look like the hell of a good fellow. "All right! Musicians, I suppose, are the antithesis of the military. If the machines approve, we'll install them and get the ships sent out. Ian Malori, I may just raise your pay." His pleasant smile broadened. "We may just have bought ourselves another standard year of life if this works out as well as I think it might."

When the machine came aboard again a few minutes later, Greenleaf bowing before it explained the essence of the plan, while Malori in the background, in an agony of terror, found himself bowing too.

"Proceed, then," the machine approved. "If you are not swift, the ship infected with life may find concealment in the storms that rise ahead of us." Then it went away again quickly. Probably it had repairs and refitting to accomplish on its own robotic ship.

With two men working, installation went very fast. It was only a matter of opening a fighting ship's cabin, inserting an uncased persona in the installed adapter, snapping together standard connectors and clamps, and closing the cabin hatch again. Since haste was vital to the berserkers' plans, testing was restricted to listening for a live response from each persona as it was activated inside a ship. Most of the responses were utter banalities about nonexistent weather or ancient food or drink, or curious phrases that Malori knew were only phatic social remarks.

All seemed to be going well, but Greenleaf was

having some last minute misgivings. "I hope these sensitive gentlemen will stand up under the strain of finding out their true situation. They will be able to grasp that, won't they? The machines won't expect them to fight well, but we don't want them going catatonic, either."

Malori, close to exhaustion, was tugging at the hatch of Number Eight, and nearly fell off the curved hull when it came open suddenly. "They will apprehend their situation within a minute after launching, I should say. At least in a general way. I don't suppose they'll understand it's interstellar space around them. You have been a military man, I suppose. If they should be reluctant to fight—I leave to you the question of how to deal with recalcitrant auxiliaries."

When they plugged the persona into ship Number Eight, its test response was: "I wish my craft to be painted red."

"At once, sir," said Malori quickly, and slammed down the ship's hatch and started to move on to Number Nine.

"What was that all about?" Greenleaf frowned, but looked at his timepiece and moved along.

"I suppose the maestro is already aware that he is about to embark in some kind of a vehicle. As to why he might like it painted red . . ." Malori grunted, trying to open up Number Nine, and let his answer trail away.

At last all the ships were ready. With his finger on the launching switch, Greenleaf paused. For one last time his eyes probed Malori's. "We've done very well, timewise. We're in for a reward, as long as this idea works at least moderately well." He was speaking now in a solemn near-whisper. "It had better work. Have you ever watched a man being skinned alive?"

Malori was gripping a stanchion to keep erect. "I have done all I can."

Greenleaf operated the launching switch. There was a polyphonic whisper of airlocks. The nine ships were gone, and simultaneously a holographic display came alive above the operations officer's console. In the center of the display the *Judith* showed as a fat green symbol, with nine smaller green dots moving slowly and uncertainly nearby. Farther off, a steady formation of red dots represented what was left of the berserker pack that had so long and so relentlessly pursued the *Hope* and her escort. There were at least fifteen red berserker dots, Malori noted gloomily.

"This trick," Greenleaf said as if to himself, "is to make them more afraid of their own leaders than they are of the enemy." He keyed the panel switches that would send his voice out to the ships. "Attention, units One through Nine!" he barked. "You are under the guns of a vastly superior force, and any attempt at disobedience or escape will be severely punished . . ."

He went on browbeating them for a minute, while Malori observed in the screen that the dirty weather the berserker had mentioned was coming on. A sleet of atomic particles was driving through this section of the nebula, across the path of the *Judith* and the odd hybrid fleet that moved with her. The *Hope*, not in view on this range scale, might be able to take advantage of the storm to get away entirely unless the berserker pursuit was swift.

Visibility on the operations display was failing fast and Greenleaf cut off his speech as it became apparent that contact was being lost. Orders in the berserkers' unnatural voices, directed at auxiliary ships One through Nine, came in fragmentarily before the curtain of noise became an opaque white-out. The pursuit of the *Hope* had not yet been resumed.

For a while all was silent on the operations deck, except for an occasional crackle of noise from the display. All around them the empty launching cradles waited.

"That's that," Greenleaf said at length. "Nothing to do now but worry." He gave his little transforming smile again, and seemed to be almost enjoying the situation.

Malori was looking at him curiously. "How do you—manage to cope so well?"

"Why not?" Greenleaf stretched and got up from the now-useless console. "You know, once a man gives up his old ways, badlife ways, admits he's really dead to them, the new ways aren't so bad. There are even women available from time to time, when the machines take prisoners."

"Goodlife," said Malori. Now he had spoken the obscene, provoking epithet. But at the moment he was not afraid.

"Goodlife yourself, little man." Greenleaf was still smiling. "You know, I think you still look down on me. You're in as deep as I am now, remember?"

"I think I pity you."

Greenleaf let out a little snort of laughter, and shook his own head pityingly. "You know, I may have ahead of me a longer and more pain-free life than most of humanity has ever enjoyed—you said one of the models for the personae died at twenty-three. Was that a common age of death in those days?"

Malori, still clinging to his stanchion, began to wear a strange, grim little smile. "Well, in his generation, in the continent of Europe, it was. The First World War was raging at the time."

"But he died of some disease, you said."

"No. I said he *had* a disease, tuberculosis. Doubtless it would have killed him eventually. But he died in battle, in 1917 CE, in a place called Belgium. His body was never found, as I recall, an artillery barrage having destroyed it and his air-craft entirely."

Greenleaf was standing very still. "Aircraft! What are you saying?"

Malori pulled himself erect, somewhat painfully, and let go of his support. "I tell you now that Georges Guynemer—that was his name—shot down fifty-three enemy aircraft before he was killed. Wait!" Malori's voice was suddenly loud and firm, and Greenleaf halted his menacing advance in sheer surprise. "Before you begin to do anything violent to me, you should perhaps consider whether your side or mine is likely to win the fight outside."

"The fight . . ."

"It will be nine ships against fifteen or more machines, but I don't feel too pessimistic. The personae we have sent out are not going to be meekly slaughtered."

Greenleaf stared at him a moment longer, then spun around and lunged for the operations console. The display was still blank white with noise and there was nothing to be done. He slowly sank into the padded chair. "What have you done to me?" he whispered. "That collection of invalid musicians—you couldn't have been lying about them all."

"Oh, every word I spoke was true. Not all World War One fighter pilots were invalids, of course. Some were in perfect health, indeed fanatical about staying that way. And I did not say they were all musicians, though I certainly meant you to think so. Ball had the most musical ability among the aces, but was still only an amateur. He always said he loathed his real profession."

Greenleaf, slumped in the chair now, seemed to be aging visibly. "But one was blind . . . it isn't possible."

"So his enemies thought, when they released him from an internment camp early in the war. Edward Mannock, blind in one eye. He had to trick an examiner to get into the army. Of course the tragedy of these superb men is that they spent themselves killing one another. In those days they had no beserkers to fight, at least none that could be attacked dashingly, with an aircraft and a machine gun. I suppose men have always faced berserkers of some kind."

"Let me make sure I understand." Greenleaf's voice was almost pleading. "We have sent out the personae of nine fighter pilots?"

"Nine of the best. I suppose their total of claimed aerial victories is more than five hundred. Such claims were usually exaggerated, but still . . ."

There was silence again. Greenleaf slowly turned his chair back to face the operations display. After a time the storm of atomic noise began to abate. Malori, who had sat down on the deck to rest, got up again, this time more quickly. In the hologram a single glowing symbol was emerging from the noise, fast approaching the position of the *Judith*.

The approaching symbol was bright red.

"So there we are," said Greenleaf, getting to his feet. From a pocket he produced a stubby little handgun. At first he pointed it toward the shrinking Malori, but then he smiled his nice smile and shook his head. "No, let the machines have you. That will be much worse."

When they heard the airlock begin to cycle, Greenleaf raised the weapon to point at his own skull. Malori could not tear his eyes away. The inner door clicked and Greenleaf fired.

Malori bounded across the intervening space and pulled the gun from Greenleaf's dead hand almost before the body had completed its fall. He turned to aim the weapon at the airlock as its inner door sighed open. The berserker standing there was the one he had seen earlier, or the same type at least. But it had just been through violent alterations. One metal arm was cut short in a bright bubbly scar, from which the ends of truncated cables flapped. The whole metal body was riddled with small holes, and around its top there played a halo of electrical discharge.

Malori fired, but the machine ignored the impact of the forcepacket. They would not have let Greenleaf keep a gun with which they could be hurt. The battered machine ignored Malori too, for the moment, and lurched forward to bend over Greenleaf's nearly decapitated body.

"Tra-tra-tra-treason," the berserker squeaked. "Ultimate unpleasant ultimate unpleasant stum-stum-stimuli. Badlife badlife bad—"

By then Malori had moved up close behind it and thrust the muzzle of the gun into one of the still-hot holes where Albert Ball or perhaps Frank Luke or Werner Voss or one of the others had already used a laser to good effect. Two forcepackets beneath its armor and the berserker went down, as still as the men who lay beneath it. The halo of electricity died.

Malori backed off, looking at them both, then spun around to scan the operations display again. The red dot was drifting away from the *Judith*, the vessel it represented now evidently no more than inert machinery.

Out of the receding atomic storm a single green dot was approaching. A minute later, Number Eight came in along, bumping to a gentle stop against its cradle pads. The laser nozzle at once began smoking heavily in atmosphere. The craft was scarred in several places by enemy fire.

"I claim four more victories," the persona said as soon as Malori opened the hatch. "Today I was given fine support by my wingmen, who made great sacrifices for the Fatherland. Although the enemy outnumbered us by two to one, I think that not a single one of them escaped. But I must protest bitterly that my aircraft still has not been painted red."

"I will see to it at once, *meinherr*," murmured Malori, as he began to disconnect the persona from the fighting ship. He felt a little foolish for trying to reassure a piece of hardware. Still, he handled the persona gently as he carried it to where the little formation of empty cases were waiting on the operations deck, their labels showing plainly:

ALBERT BALL;

WILLIAM AVERY BISHOP;

RENE PAUL FONCK;

GEORGES MARIE GUYNEMER;

FRANK LUKE;

EDWARD MANNOCK:

CHARLES NUNGESSER:

MANFRED VON RICHTHOFEN:

WERNER VOSS.

They were English, American, German, French. They were Jew, violinist, invalid, Prussian, rebel, hater, bon vivant, Christian. Among the nine of them they were many other things besides. Maybe there was only the one word—man—which could include them all.

Right now the nearest living humans were many millions of kilometers away, but still Malori did not feel quite alone. He put the persona back into its case gently, even knowing that it would be undamaged by ten thousand more gravities than his hands could exert. Maybe it would fit into the cabin of Number Eight with him, when he made his try to reach the *Hope*.

"Looks like it's just you and me now, Red Baron." The human being from which it had been modeled had been not quite twenty-six when he was killed over France, after less than eighteen months of success and fame. Before that, in the cavalry, his horse had thrown him again and again.

FRED SABERHAGEN

Fred Saberhagen needs very little introduction these days. His most famous creations—the awesome Berserkers—are known to SF readers around the world. He's reached the bestseller lists several times, most recently with his "Book of Swords" series, and his novels span the territory from hard science fiction to high fantasy. Quite understandably, Saberhagen's been labeled one of the best writers in the business.

These fine novels by Saberhagen are available from Baen Books:

PYRAMIDS
A fascinating new twist on the time-travel novel, introducing a great new series hero: Pilgrim, the Flying Dutchman of Time, whose only hope for returning home lies in subtly altering the history of our own timeline to more closely reflect his own. Fortunately for us, Pilgrim's timeline is a rather more pleasant one than ours, and so the changes are—or at least are supposed to be—for the better. Learn why the curse of the Pharaoh Khufu (builder of the Great Pyramid) had a special reality, in *Pyramids*. "Saberhagen's light, imaginative and enjoyable adventures speed along twisting paths to a climax that is even more surprising than the rest of the book." —*Publishers Weekly*

AFTER THE FACT
This is the second novel featuring the great new series hero, Pilgrim—the Lost Traveller adrift in time and dimensionality. His current project: to rescue Abraham Lincoln from assassination, AFTER THE FACT!

THE FRANKENSTEIN PAPERS
At last—the truth about the sinister Dr. Frankenstein and his monster with a heart of gold, based on a history written by the monster himself! Find out what happened when the mad Doctor brought his creation to life, and why the monster has no scars.

THE "EMPIRE OF THE EAST" SERIES
THE BROKEN LANDS, Book I
A masterful blend of high technology and high sorcery; a unique adventure in a world on the brink of ultimate change; a world were magic rules—and science struggles to live again! *"Empire of the East* is one of the best science fiction fantasy epics—Saberhagen can be justly proud. Highly recommended."—*Science Fiction Review*. "A fine mix of fantasy and science fiction, action and speculation."—Roger Zelazny

THE BLACK MOUNTAINS, Book II
East meets West in bloody conflict on a world where magic rules, but technology is revolting! *"Empire of the East* is the work of a master!"—*Magazine of Fantasy and Science Fiction*

ARDNEH'S WORLD, Book III
The gripping climax of the "Empire of the East" series. "Ranks favorably with Tolkien. Exceptional in sheer unbridled zest and imaginative sweep."
—*School Library Journal*

* * *

THE GOLDEN PEOPLE
Genetically perfect, super-human children are created by a dedicated scientist for the betterment of Mankind. As the children mature, however, they begin to wonder if Man *should* survive . . .

LOVE CONQUERS ALL
In a future where childbirth is outlawed and promiscuity required, one woman dares fight the system for the right to bear children.

MY BEST
Saberhagen presents his personal best, in *My Best*. One sure to please lovers of "hard" science fiction as well as high fantasy.

OCTAGON
Players scattered across the continent are engaged in a game called "Starweb." Each player has certain attributes, and can ally with or attack any of the others. But one player seems to have confused the reality of the world: a player with the attributes of machinelike precision and mechanical ruthlessness. His name is Octagon, and he's out for blood.

You can order all of Fred Saberhagen's books with this order form. Check your choices and send the combined cover price/s to: Baen Books, Dept. BA, 260 Fifth Avenue, New York, New York 10001.

PYRAMIDS • 320 pp. •
65609-0 • $3.50   _____
AFTER THE FACT • 320 pp. •
65391-1 • $3.95   _____
THE FRANKENSTEIN PAPERS •
288 pp. • 65550-7 • $3.50   _____
THE BROKEN LANDS • 224 pp. •
65380-6 • $2.95   _____
THE BLACK MOUNTAINS • 192 pp.
• 65390-3 • $2.75   _____
ARDNEH'S WORLD, Book III •
192 pp. • 65404-7 • $2.75   _____
THE GOLDEN PEOPLE • 272 pp. •
55904-4 • $3.50   _____
LOVE CONQUERS ALL • 288 pp. •
55953-2 • $2.95   _____
MY BEST • 320 pp. • 65645-7 •
$2.95   _____
OCTAGON • 288 pp. •
65353-9 • $2.95

Have You Missed?

DRAKE, DAVID
At Any Price
Hammer's Slammers are back—and Baen Books has them!
Now the 23rd-century armored division faces its deadliest
enemies ever: aliens who *teleport* into combat.
55978-8 $3.50

DRAKE, DAVID
Hammer's Slammers
A special *expanded* edition of the book that began the
legend of Colonel Alois Hammer. Now the toughest, mean-
est mercs who ever killed for a dollar or wrecked a world
for pay have come home—to Baen Books—and they've
brought a secret weapon: "The Tank Lords," a brand-new
short novel, included in this special Baen edition of *Hammer's Slammers*. **65632-5 $3.50**

DRAKE, DAVID
Lacey and His Friends
In Jed Lacey's time the United States computers scan
every citizen, every hour of the day. When crime is de-
tected, it's Lacey's turn. There are a few things worse than
having him come after you, but they're not survivable
either. But things aren't really that bad—not for Lacey and
his friends. By the author of *Hammer's Slammers* and *At
Any Price*. **65593-0 $3.50**

**CARD, ORSON SCOTT; DRAKE, DAVID;
& BUJOLD, LOIS MCMASTER**
(edited by Elizabeth Mitchell)
Free Lancers (Alien Stars, Vol. IV)
Three short novels about mercenary soldiers—never be-
fore in print! Card's hero leads a ragtag group of scientific
refugees to sanctuary in Utah; Drake contributes a new
"Hammer's Slammers" story; Bujold tells a new tale of
Miles Vorkosigan, hero of *The Warrior's Apprentice*.
65352-0 $2.95

DRAKE, DAVID
Birds of Prey
The time: 262 A.D. The place: Imperial Rome. There had never been a greater empire, but now it is dying. Everywhere its armies are in retreat, and what had been civilization seethes with riots and bizarre cults. Against the imminent fall of the Long Night stands Aulus Perennius, an Imperial secret agent as tough and ruthless as the age in which he lives. But he stands alone—until a traveller from Earth's far future recruits him for a mission so strange it cannot be disclosed.

55912-5 (trade paper) $7.95
55909-5 (hardcover) $14.95

DRAKE, DAVID
Ranks of Bronze
Disguised alien traders bought captured Roman soldiers on the slave market because they needed troops who could win battles without high-tech weaponry. The leigionaires provided victories, smashing barbarian armies with the swords, javelins, and discipline that had won a world. But the worlds on which they now fought were strange ones, and the spoils of victory did not include freedom. If the legionaires went home, it would be through the use of the beam weapons and force screens of their ruthless alien owners. It's been 2000 years—and now they want to go home.   65568-X $3.50

DRAKE, DAVID, & WAGNER, KARL EDWARD
Killer
Vonones and Lycon capture wild animals to sell for bloodsport in ancient Rome. A vicious animal sold to them by a trader turns out to be more than they bargained for—it is the sole survivor of the crash of an alien spacecraft. Possessed of intelligence nearly human, it has two goals in life: to breed and to kill.

55931-1 $2.95

DAVID DRAKE

"Drake has distinguished himself as the master of the mercenary sf novel."—Rave Reviews